Tigers of the Ice

A fictional story based on the true experiences of

Dr. Elisha Kane

By

Charles Patton

Tigers of the Ice

Notice

This story is inspired by true events. However, dialogue and certain events and characters in this work are the product of the author's imagination or are used fictitiously. This is not a historical account but only a dramatization of an amazing story of survival and death.

This fictional story is built around the true experiences of Dr. Elisha Kane. Dr. Kane and his men lived in an era when, for the most part, men were much tougher than most are today!

This novel is rooted in historical facts and uses the term 'Esquimaux' to accurately reflect the language of the time for Indigenous Arctic residents, now correctly referred to as 'Inuit'. This choice is not intended to uphold outdated or disrespectful views, and the depiction of Esquimaux characters is respectful.

We also use the historical term "sledge" as they did to refer to their dog sleds.

Short Mystery Press
ISBN: 978-1-963809-53-4
 (IngSprkPB)
Written for and sponsored by:
Applied Market Solutions, LLC
6045 Lexington Park
Orlando, FL 32819

The book that inspired this work of fiction is: "Arctic Explorations, the Second Grinnell Expedition, in search of Sir John Franklin 1853, '54, '55 by Elisha Kent Kane, M.D., U.S.N., Vol I and II," Philadelphia, Childs & Peterson, 124 Arch Street, et alia, 1856.

All the line drawings are from Kane's original text and, I believe, drawn by him except his portrait which was credited to R. Whitechurch.
Book template by usedtotech.com.
Polar Bear image courtesy of William Curtis Rolf.
Role of Artificial Intelligence (AI) in this book: I found OpenAI's chatGPT™ Ver 4.2 useful in cleaning up, simplifying, fleshing out, rearranging my dyslexic sentences, and researching sources. I am responsible for all the writing.

In "Tigers of the Ice," Arctic polar bears are likened to tigers, symbolizing their mastery over harsh environments and status at the top of their food chains. This metaphor underscores their shared tenacity and alludes to Dr. Elisha Kent Kane's crew's strength and resilience in the Arctic. The polar bear also emerges as a spiritual intermediary, linking the Arctic's elemental forces, the Esquimaux and Kane's explorers, representing a profound bond between humans, nature, and the Arctic's mystique.

CONTENTS

Introduction

In the frigid heart of the Arctic, where the world's edges blur and the icy abyss stretches endlessly, a realm beckons to the souls of intrepid adventurers and fearless explorers. It is a place where the very air crackles with mystery, and the shimmering Northern Lights sing like a celestial chorus to the tales of hardship and heroism.

Welcome to a world of perilous ambition and relentless determination, where the names John Franklin and Doctor Elisah Kane echo through the frozen corridors of time. In this story of Arctic exploration, we embark on a journey that transcends the boundaries of human ambition.

It is 1853. Doctor Elisah Kane is bound northward to learn the fate of Sir John Franklin, a veteran seafarer who vanished sis years earlier in pursuit of the Northwest Passage—a sea route through the ice-bound islands of northern Canada, long whispered of but never traversed. Promising swifter trade to the Orient, it was a path beset with peril, legend, and ice.

In 1845, Franklin and 128 men aboard the HMS Erebus and the HMS Terror sailed into the polar silence. They never returned. By 1847, rescue parties had followed, each battling the elements for answers, each returning with none.

Doctor Kane's expedition would face the same cruel wilderness: icebergs grinding against timbered hulls, predators hidden in snowdrifts, and frost that crept into bone and spirit alike. Yet amid the privation, bonds were forged—quiet acts of loyalty and endurance in a land where survival was never certain.

This is the record of Dr. Kane's search, and of the enduring mystery of Franklin's fate.

I. Arctic Whispers and Roars

Beneath the flapping canvas of his two-man tent on the ice of Davis Strait, Dr. Elisha Kane bent over a small table, diligently recording his day's findings. The U.S. Navy had assigned him to assist the Canadian government in surveying the untouched geology in a remote area at the northern extremity of Newfoundland's northeast coast beyond the Arctic Circle. Kane. Broad-shouldered and weathered like a veteran sea captain, Kane's deep brown eyes and light hair caught the lamplight. He casually wore his navy-blue pea coat open, and his wool cap rakishly tilted back on his head in the low-teen temperatures.

From his vantage point on the icy shoreline, Kane gazed upon a mesmerizing landscape of rolling hummocks and towering blocks of ice, their colors shifting between translucent blue and stark white. Some reached staggering heights of up to 15 feet, chaotically strewn as far as the eye could see. The Arctic horizon glowed with the muted orange of a setting sun, casting its waning light across the camp. This ethereal light gently brushed Kane's sledge, and the dogs tethered nearby, dusting them in shades of deep violet and burnished gold.

Out of the stillness, a harrowing scream echoed, swiftly followed by a guttural roar that shattered Kane's moment of solitude.

Without hesitation, he sprang from his stool, snatching his Marston rifle, and sprinted toward the alarming noise, weaving through the ice.

A chaotic fray burst into view as he came around a massive, ten-foot-tall ice block. A juvenile polar bear relentlessly attacked Henri Bellot, Kane's French-Canadian compatriot, landing forceful blows with its massive paws upon Henri's shoulders and flanks. With a swift, fierce swipe, the bear sent Henri's elongated knit hat flying, narrowly missing his head as he dodged the strike. Rearing up on its hind legs, even though young, the bear towered over Henri, who stood at a modest five-foot-four.

"Hold on, Henri," Kane shouted. "I'm here."

Pinned beneath the bear's weight, Henri pushed upwards against its chin, fiercely struggling until he slipped free, tumbling backward. In a swift move, the bear pounced, sinking its teeth into Henri's thigh. Finding no clear line of fire, Kane discarded his rifle and snatched a harpoon from Henri's nearby sledge.

Swinging the harpoon by its shaft, Kane struck the bear's head with the blunt end, intentionally avoiding the weapon's lethal point. Undeterred, the bear shook its head like a wet dog shedding water.

In the continuing battle, Kane received shallow claw marks across his chest after diverting the bear's attention from Henri. Kane took another swing at the bear with the harpoon's handle, but it went wide. In its retaliatory lunge, the bear impaled itself on the harpoon's tip, the blade sinking partially into its chest. Locked in a fierce embrace, Kane and the bear wrestled, their blood intertwining and dripping on the icy ground. Then, the bear abruptly released Kane and retreated, leaving him stunned and panting.

Kane held firm, eyes locked on the receding bear. Henri, gathering his strength, managed to crawl and then, shakily, get to his feet. He made his way to where Kane's discarded rifle lay, retrieved it, and, positioning himself beside Kane, aimed at the departing beast.

Shaking from the adrenaline and exertion, Henri knelt, resting his left elbow on his knee for a steadier shot. But just as his finger began to apply pressure to the trigger, Kane, looming over him, seized the rifle's barrel, jerking it upwards. The unexpected motion sent Henri sprawling backward, the shot discharging harmlessly into the sky.

"I had him in my sights," Henri exclaimed, voice tinged with disbelief. "Why did you stop me? That beast almost took my life!"

Kane, his hand instinctively resting on the fresh claw marks across his chest, watched as the bear vanished into the labyrinth of icy mounds. Henri remained on his knees, breath ragged. With a steadying hand on Henri's shoulder, Kane anchored him as they both witnessed the bear's fading silhouette.

As the bear disappeared, Kane withdrew his hand, extending the other to help Henri to his feet. Once upright, Henri retrieved a whisky flask from inside his coat, punctured by a bear's claw. He sipped from the rivulet of amber liquid escaping the gash.

"But he didn't. Now, we're all survivors," Kane said.

"When did you start showing charity towards bears?" "Incredulous," Henri murmured as they retraced their steps to their camp.

As they rounded the final hummock before their camp, a jarring sight confronted them: nearly all their belongings—the sledge, dogs, table, and supplies—had vanished. Only the empty tent stood, its flaps billowing in the wind. Kane's journal lay discarded on the ice, its pages ruffling in the wind's embrace. Further north, they could see two Esquimaux rapidly pulling Kane's possessions on his sledge, drawn by his dogs.

Kane relieved Henri of the rifle, squinting down its barrel. Henri gave a discouraging shake of his head. Understanding the distance and their scarce ammunition, Kane decided against taking the shot. Their predicament grew more dire with Kane's scratches and Henri's injuries from the bear encounter.

Left with only Henri's sledge and dogs, a rifle with a single moisture-sensitive cartridge, and no food, fuel, or means to produce drinkable water, their journey to the nearest settlement pushed them to the brink of death. While they survived, the harrowing ordeals Kane and Henri faced during this trip left Kane with deep-seated resentment towards the Esquimaux, whom he saw as threats on par with the perils of navigating ice, polar bears, and enduring frigid temperatures.

Yet from his Arctic experiences, Kane found solace and an idea that sparked an unquenchable thirst for adventure. Driven by curiosity and the Arctic's allure, he envisioned leading an audacious expedition to uncover Sir John Franklin's enigmatic fate in the frigid Arctic wilderness, taking two years to germinate fully.

II. Siren's Calls

Dr. Elisha Kane

A few years had elapsed since Kane's Arctic experiences and honorable discharge from the Navy, where he had attained the rank of captain. Yet, the lure of the North remained. During these years, he took it upon himself to embark on a perilous mission he had envisioned on the Davis Strait—borne from an unshakeable determination that sprang from within.

This mission carried the weight of history and mystery—a British explorer, the esteemed Sir John Franklin, had ventured into the unknown, vanishing without a trace along with 129 brave souls and two sturdy ships. Their destination lay near Baffin Bay or somewhere farther west, nestled within the Arctic Circle, south and west of Greenland.

Silence had enveloped Franklin's expedition for almost four years, extinguishing the once-burning flames of hope. In its place, a groundswell of determination rose in England and the United States, demanding an expedition to confirm their loss and unearth any fragment of evidence that could be salvaged from the frozen north.

With his seasoned experience in the unforgiving northern realms, Kane believed he possessed the qualifications to spearhead a perilous search endeavor. Yet, he understood the bitter truth that clung to the expedition's frigid trail—little hope remained of discovering any of the men alive. And yet, he went ahead, driven by an unyielding spirit and sense of duty, willing to again confront the chilling unknown and its secrets concealed in the Arctic wilderness.

In the brisk early spring of 1853, Dr. Kane found himself in the grand lobby of the Department of the Navy's headquarters in Washington. He stood there, momentarily transfixed, lost in contemplation, his gaze fixated on a magnificent display that dominated the room, featuring a towering twelve-foot-tall polar bear mounted upright. Time seemed to slow as he stood there, absorbing every detail of this immense, fearsome, and mysterious creature frozen in time. Slowly, he shook his head as if attempting to dispel a haunting memory that clung to his thoughts. His eyes then ascended to meet the great bear's head, its mighty jaws agape, teeth bared, and lips twisted in a fearsome snarl. The sight sent shivers down his spine, and for a moment, it transported him back to the chilling encounter with the smaller bear that had once threatened Henri, his companion on a previous expedition.

Though fashioned from glass, the massive bear's eyes possessed an uncanny lifelike quality. They were as dark and penetrating as Kane's own, two orbs containing the secrets of the frigid wilderness.

As he stood there, locked in a silent exchange with the beast, he felt an unsettling connection, as if the spirit of the Arctic had found a way to peer into his soul through those unyielding, glassy eyes.

The exhibition, meticulously curated by the Smithsonian Institute in collaboration with the Department of the Navy, extended beyond the towering polar bear display. It unfolded a captivating array of scientific instruments, each bearing witness to the indomitable spirit of Arctic exploration and the imperative quest for survival during long, treacherous voyages.

Among the displayed exploration treasures was the theodolite, a precise instrument that held the power to survey and measure heights and distances with unwavering accuracy. It was the sentinel of precision in the icy wilderness, an instrument relied upon for charting the unknown, one of Kane's objectives.

Adjacent to the theodolite, the sextant stood as a testament to the artistry of navigation. Its elegant design masked its essential role—to measure the angle of the sun, which would reveal latitude in the uncharted expanses of the Arctic. In its simplicity, the sextant could unveil a ship's distance between the equator and the north pole – fixing the ship's location in vast expanses of water and icy wasteland.

The chronometer, a modest timepiece with a crucial role in celestial observation, was the key to determining longitude. The chromometer was essential for navigating uncharted waters in the vastness of the icy wilderness, where time and space merged. The ship would soon be lost without them unless the navigator could recognize landmarks. Navigational charts were inaccurate when getting to the Arctic and non-existent in the farthest north. The timepieces required daily winding, where failure to do so could cause the ship to be steered astray. The chronometer was, quite simply, their reliable time compass, pointing the way back to the safety of the known world.

Kane understood that Arctic navigation demanded a careful blend of art and science. These three instruments, laid out meticulously before him, bridged the gap between human ingenuity and the unforgiving wilderness. They were the practical tools, each holding the promise of discovery and the prospect of a safe return from the icy heart of the far Arctic.

Returning abruptly from his brief reverie, Kane adjusted his attire, preparing himself for the upcoming presentation. In his well-worn navy pea-coat, white shirt, and tie, he smoothed a few stray locks of prematurely graying hair, pushing them back beneath a snug, dark navy blue knit cap. With a glance at his pocket watch, a last check of the letter folio cradled under his arm, he hastened towards the wide, winding staircase, ready to make his case to the Secretary of the Navy and one of his senior aides.

Upon reaching the top floor, Kane was warmly received by the navy Secretary's elderly, silver-haired receptionist. She had been expecting and promptly guided him into a spacious office adorned with rich mahogany paneling and maritime embellishments. On one wall, newspaper front pages chronicled the Franklin expedition's journey to the Arctic in 1845, each showing the same pre-embarkation engraving depicting Sir Franklin, his officers, and their intrepid crew. Nearby, other headlines told a somber tale—announcing government speculations of their mysterious disappearance in 1847 and later issues describing the fruitless search efforts that unfolded between 1848 and 1852, leaving Franklin's fate shrouded in uncertainty. None of those rescue efforts located his ships or men.

"Dr. Kane, it's a pleasure to make your acquaintance," the Secretary greeted with a genial smile. "Do you know Mr. Grinnell?"

The Secretary cut a dignified figure, the epitome of a meticulous government official. His salt-and-pepper hair elegantly cascaded over his collar, mirroring his neatly groomed mustache. His attire, impeccably aligned with the fashion of the era, featured a starched, round-cornered pleated shirt, a small bow tie artfully folded on the diagonal and fastened in a winged knot, a frockcoat, and a double-breasted waistcoat, cut with a precision that mirrored his overall demeanor.

"No, sir, but I sailed under one of his captains, Captain Haven, during Mr. Grinnell's Greenland expedition two years ago," Dr. Kane said.

Mr. Grinnell's attire and demeanor exuded opulence and affluence. He adorned himself in a pristine cutaway morning coat paired with impeccably tailored striped trousers embellished with braid trimming down the sides. His shirt featured a crisply starched, short, straight collar, perfectly complementing his ensemble. He sported half boots with discreet yet stylishly short heels to complete the picture of sartorial splendor. His well-groomed grey hair added a touch of refinement to his appearance.

"And here we have Admiral Hall, my capable assistant for naval operations," the Secretary introduced, his words carrying an air of respect.

Admiral Hall's attire exuded formality, distinguished by a profusion of brass buttons and ornate fringe epaulets. A splendid dress sword embellished with an ivory grip at his side emitted an aura of regal authority. Kane couldn't help but take note of the admiral's relatively youthful appearance, which contrasted with his high-ranking position, intriguing him further.

The Secretary, gesturing with a stack of official-looking letters, continued, "Though we hold no illusions about Franklin's survival, we are compelled to bring closure to this matter for his wife, Lady Jane Franklin. Please present your proposal for our consideration."

The Secretary and Grinnell made their way to a modest table and took their seats while Dr. Kane improvised his presentation by unpinning a sizable map from the wall, a grand-scale chart of the region. The admiral, adopting a commanding posture akin to one on the bridge of a ship, paced about the room with a purposeful air.

With great care, Kane placed the expansive map on the table. He then produced a smaller map of his own, portraying the southern stretches of Greenland and the western portion of Newfoundland. Despite their differences in size, these maps bore a striking resemblance, each marked by vast, untouched swaths of white space labeled simply as "unexplored."

As Kane paced in tandem with the admiral, he paused intermittently to draw their attention to key features on both maps, using his words and gestures to illuminate the path of their shared journey into the unknown.

"My plan calls for us to follow the western coast of Greenland north to the extent weather and ice allow," Kane said. "From there, as far as boats and sledges can penetrate, we will search coastlines and the interior for signs of the lost party."

As Kane traced his intended course on the map with his finger, Grinnell interjected with a probing question.

"What gives you the confidence to believe you can succeed where others, with more extensive experience, have faltered?" he inquired pointedly. "After all, you've never helmed your own vessel despite attaining the rank of captain."

"I once served as the first officer under a captain renowned for delegation," Kane began with unwavering confidence. "My persistence, however, sets me apart, and my plan hinges on a crucial distinction," he continued. "When we venture into the northern reaches of Greenland, our approach will shift. We'll embark on our searches from a solid land base, mitigating the unpredictability of ice travel."

"How do you intend to sustain your party for twelve to fifteen months?" Grinnell inquired, his skepticism evident.

Kane's response was prompt and resolute. "We'll rely on hunting expeditions, utilizing both foot and sledge parties," he explained.

Grinnell began to mention the presence of Esquimaux colonies as far north as—

But Kane interjected with a sense of urgency, his determination to clarify his plan.

"Placing our survival in the hands of the Esquimaux would be a perilous gamble," he asserted firmly. "Their disposition is fraught with hostility, unpredictability, and danger. I would never place my trust in the Esquimaux for any critical endeavor. Even those few who have assimilated into society retain a childlike and unreliable nature."

"Surviving, as they do, in the harshest corner of the earth, perhaps nature has forged them into what they are," Admiral Hall mused.

Kane was resolute in his response. "We won't rely on them for our survival," he reaffirmed.

Grinnell's tone hardened. "We're not in the business of sponsoring reckless or suicidal escapades," he emphasized. "What drives you to seek out such perilous risks?"

"For the sake of Sir Franklin and his men's families," Kane replied unwaveringly. "To offer them solace and peace of mind."

The Secretary turned to Grinnell, silently seeking his approval. In response, Grinnell offered a subtle, fleeting nod, his lips curling into a brief grin, a rare display of agreement.

"Very well," the Secretary conceded. "Mr. Grinnell will make the brig Advance available under your command. The Navy will furnish six dedicated volunteers, along with a year's worth of supplies and rations."

Grinnell voiced their unwavering support, stating, "The Smithsonian will shoulder the expenses for the remainder of your crew and provisions."

The Secretary, however, added a crucial disclaimer, his tone carrying a note of caution.

"It's vital you understand the Navy's position. It's regarded as a private venture, bound by private rules. We will not be at your beck and call, and if you share Franklin's fate, no rescue will come."

Pausing briefly to ensure he hadn't omitted any crucial details, the Secretary continued, "This plan offers no adventure, only an abundance of hardship. Will you embark on this journey under these terms?"

Both pleased and confident, Kane recognized the perils that lay ahead and wasted no time expressing his acceptance. "I will, sir," he affirmed, sealing his commitment to the endeavor.

"Then, Godspeed and fair weather," Grinnell said.

Kane shook Grinnell's and the admiral's hands. The Secretary showed Kane out.

As Dr. Kane made his way toward the exit, the Secretary halted him with a gentle grasp on his arm, preventing his departure.

"Mr. Brooks, who sailed alongside you on your previous voyage, will oversee the Navy's preparations," the Secretary informed him. "I recommend considering him as your first officer. His experience may complement any gaps in your own. Additionally, the institute insists on sending their astronomer, August Sontag, with you. I assume you would also have no objections to enlisting some of the Advance's previous crew members. They'll be ready to board next Monday, at which point you may assume command. Farewell."

Kane once again shook the Secretary's hand, expressing his gratitude.

The Secretary then handed Kane an envelope. "Take these as well," he said. "They carry the Danish ambassador's letters of introduction, authority for your presence in their waters, and directives for Greenland's settlements to provide you with supplies. These might prove useful if you are met with any resistance."

"Thank you for the trust you've bestowed upon me," Dr. Kane responded, to which the Secretary nodded in acknowledgment.

After Kane turned and walked away, the Secretary stood watching him, slightly shaking his head because he knew some of the dangers Kane would face and could imagine many more.

The Secretary mumbled to himself, "I hope this isn't the last time we see him."

As Kane stepped into the corridor, he came dangerously close to a collision OBURSTwith his old companion from the bear attack, Henri Bellot. Adorned in his resplendent Canadian Naval captain's uniform, Henri was in a hurry, clutching a letter folio beneath his arm, much like the one Kane carried.

"Well, if it isn't Captain Bellot!" Kane greeted him with a warm smile.

"Mon ami!" Bellot exclaimed, his face lighting up. "It's been too long since Davis Strait. You're looking much more robust than the last time I saw you. Any plans for another northern expedition?"

Kane chuckled, recognizing the allure of the Arctic all too well. "You know how irresistible that Northern siren can be," he admitted. "Indeed, I'm on the verge of embarking on a search for Sir Franklin."

Bellot waved his portfolio.

"Bon!" Bellot exclaimed. "Then our missions align. Today, I seek sponsorship from your Navy and my country's Maritime Commission for an expedition to find Franklin and his party—venturing northeast from the Newfoundland coast."

Kane contemplated the prospect. "Our paths may not intersect on that course," he replied thoughtfully. "Can the 'Polaris' withstand another journey through the icy regions?"

Bellot continued walking, preoccupied, his voice trailing off as he entered the Secretary's office, leaving Kane alone in the corridor.

"Just launched a new clipper, 'The Bear Hunter,'" Bellot's voice echoed from inside the office. "With a new ship and some luck, maybe I'll make a name for myself. The race is on, Mon Ami. Bon voyage!"

Kane offered a parting wave to Bellot's receding form, even though his companion had already disappeared into the Secretary's office. He then resumed his solitary journey down the corridor, his muttered words echoing as if Bellot were still by his side.

"You're preoccupied with fame, but..." Kane's voice trailed off as he continued his internal monologue. "Reaching the North is the easy part. It's the return that poses the true challenge. The ice, the bone-chilling cold, and the enigmatic Esquimaux may conspire to hold you captive in that frozen realm, possibly forever. No doubt they'll try the same with us."

Over the following weeks, Kane assembled the crew he had carefully chosen and those assigned to him, gathered the necessary supplies, provisions, and equipment, and had everything readied for his impending voyage on the Advance. Once he was fully organized, with his seasoned crew and all materials awaiting him at the dock, he made his way to the ship. The Advance, a rugged vessel with a storied history etched into its weathered timbers, stood as a testament to its countless expeditions into the unknown. As he approached, the mantle of leadership settled upon his shoulders, and the Arctic winds whispered secrets known only to those brave enough to listen.

III. Kane in Command

A few weeks later, in the dim, smoke-hazed confines of the Rusty Anchor—a dockside tavern beloved by Annapolis' roughest salts—Samuel Godfrey, tall and sinewy with fiery red hair, hunched over a modest table. His soot-covered appearance could rival that of a diligent chimney sweep. The Rusty Anchor was a sanctuary for the salty souls who frequented Annapolis' rugged docks.

Empty shot glasses and beer mugs lay scattered before him, proof of the drunkenness he and Riley had eagerly embraced. Riley, a lean sailor with a sharp nose and angular features, sat opposite Godfrey, his twitching nose betraying a restless nature. His appearance was unkempt, and he kept sniffing the air without pause.

"Are you thinking of mutiny at some point in the voyage?" Riley asked.

Godfrey stared at him, "You think I would tell you if I was?"

Godfrey, his gaze fixed on a weathered bucket strategically placed to catch raindrops from the leaky ceiling, tossed back another shot with practiced ease. He then nonchalantly retrieved his short-billed hat adorned with an eagle-over-anchor badge, a symbol reminiscent of a ship's captain, and flung it into the bucket. The impact knocked the bucket askew, sending water splattering across the floor, though nobody in the establishment seemed to care.

With unsteady determination, Godfrey reached into his pocket, pulled out, and tugged on a dark navy blue knit cap, fitting it snugly over his head. He pushed himself up from the table, swaying as he stood, and began a staggered journey toward the exit. Only when he observed Godfrey making a beeline for the door did Riley abruptly abandon his seat and follow, scurrying in his companion's unsteady wake.

As the sun emerged from its morning hideaway behind rain clouds, it cast a luminous glow over the late spring landscape, gradually dispelling the remnants of puddles created by the earlier downpour. Dr. Kane, wearing a captain's hat like the one Godfrey had tossed into the bucket, rounded the street corner, and beheld his majestic vessel, the Advance. It stood resolute at her dock, though nearly concealed from sight by an assortment of cargo—stacks of crates, burlap sacks, tins, barrels, wood, and canvas, among other things.

In the bustling hive of activity that enveloped the scene, stevedores and crew members bustled about, pushing wheelbarrows, pulling laden carts, and heaving supplies and materials onto the ship. These provisions gradually found their temporary haven within the vessel's holds, concealed below decks.

Kane paused in the bustling street, absorbing his surroundings. At that moment, Godfrey lurched out of the saloon, heading directly toward Kane. In a half-hearted attempt to halt his momentum, Godfrey tried to push aside the figure in his path. However, despite his wiry strength, he couldn't avoid a mild jostle. Even after regaining his balance, he failed to recognize he'd bumped into Kane.

"Out of my way, landlubber!" Godfrey grumbled, his voice a perpetual rasp that underscored his gruff demeanor.

Kane pushed his hat back and shook his head, lamenting the seaman's wretched state. Recognizing that this disheveled soul was destined to be a member of his forthcoming crew, Kane trailed behind Godfrey as the man staggered toward the looming ship.

Meanwhile, Riley darted out of the tavern's doorway, his wiry form sprinting past Godfrey and Kane in a blur of urgency. He ascended the gangway hastily and descended into the ship's hold, his nimble movements showing his eagerness to get to work.

On the ship's deck, Dr. Hayes, newly appointed as the ship's surgeon, unnecessarily but willingly threw himself into loading provisions. He labored under the watchful eye of First Officer Brooks, choosing to voluntarily work alongside the crew despite being a direct to the captain.

Brooks, a formidable figure with a stout physique, sported a head of brown hair with dignified traces of gray. His neatly trimmed beard matched the subtle graying of his hair, giving him an aura of authority that extended beyond his position as the first officer. One might have surmised that Brooks was aboard not solely to fulfill his duties as Captain Kane's second-in-command but also to serve as Kane's unwavering and fiercely loyal protector.

Brooks straightened his blue woolen frock coat as he stepped forward, the deeper shade of its lined collars and lapels catching the light. Paired with matching trousers and vest, he cut a formidable figure. The white cuffs of his coat peeked out just so, and a black handkerchief was tucked neatly into his pocket. As he moved, the shine of his black buckled shoes reflected his meticulous nature.

"Put your backs to it, men!" Brooks's voice rang out, a directive aimed at no one but intended for everyone.

"We have a mountain of cargo to load and scarce time to do so."

Dr. Hayes was also sizable, but Brooks stood taller and exuded a more powerful presence. Even though the doctor was dressed more like a gentleman than a ship's officer, in a suit jacket, vest, and striped trousers, no one dared chide him about his clothes because he had the powerful arms of a surgeon. With his rugged looks, he might pass for a seaman in rougher clothes, but he lacked any experience at sea whatsoever.

Watching the slow progress, Kane's anxiety grew—any delay could cost lives. He hurried toward Brooks.

As Godfrey neared the ship, his instincts sharpened. Spotting an unattended hand truck, he grabbed it without hesitation. Dr. Hayes observed as Godfrey, wind-tousled and clearly irritable, made a slow, silent gesture calling for Brooks's help with a crate.

Always leading by example, Brooks dismissed Godfrey's weak offer to help, lifting the crate onto the hand truck alone. In turn, Godfrey, displaying his discontent, gave the box a rough kick.

"Godfrey, curb that attitude, or I'll send you back to your saloon," Brooks admonished sternly, his voice carrying the weight of authority.

Reluctantly, Godfrey resumed his task, methodically stacking boxes onto his hand truck. Crates labeled "meat-biscuit" and "dried fruit," alongside barrels marked "dried potatoes" and "pickled cabbage," littered the dock, forming an edible mosaic of provisions awaiting their voyage.

Brooks, overseeing the bustling activity, issued his next set of instructions.

Once you've stowed that stack," he began, pointing decisively to each location, "take two men and load this stack into the forward hold. Then, place that other pile aft, right next to where we stored the navy's salt beef and pork ration.

Godfrey, with years of seafaring experience shaping his instincts, couldn't help but interject. "You should be separating the dried fruits and vegetables from the pickled cabbage and salted meat," he advised.

Brooks was in no mood for argument. Amid the dock's clamor, his voice cut through—sharp and commanding. "Just put it where I tell you, Godfrey," he asserted. "This ship doesn't have the luxury of space for separating storage."

Meanwhile, in the background, a rat scampered up one of the hawsers anchoring the ship to the dock. Not long after, Riley emerged from the deck below, plunging back into the chaos above.

"Mr. Riley, take this hard biscuit and flour and follow Mr. Godfrey forward," instructed Brooks.

"Aye, sir," Riley responded, falling in behind Godfrey as he pushed a hand truck bearing two small barrels.

"Where should these be stowed?" Riley asked, his query directed to anyone within earshot.

"I'm not the captain here," Godfrey snapped, his patience waning. "Ask the one in the hat," he suggested, nodding towards Kane, who stood by Brooks near the ship's wheel.

But even with Godfrey's curt dismissal, Riley persisted, trailing him, hoping for answers.

Under Brooks and Kane's watchful eyes, the ship buzzed with activity, shedding its calm appearance. Kane moved forward, inspecting the cargo, while Dr. Hayes approached Brooks—the seasoned first officer known for his steady hand at sea.

"I don't have a lot of sea experience," Hayes admitted, "but I'd be happy to assist with loading the pemmican. We're talking about two thousand pounds, right?"

"Yes," Brooks replied. "Proceed."

"And, if I might add," Dr. Hayes continued, "that Godfrey fellow seems particularly surly."

Brooks responded with a knowing smile. "He has his reasons," he acknowledged. "Before our commissions, Godfrey was the first officer on this ship. Dr. Kane's arrival displaced him, thwarting his aspirations of captaincy. When I joined the crew and assumed the first officer role, it left him nowhere to ascend. However, to give credit where it's due, we did elevate him to chief mate, the most prestigious rank above seaman at this wharf."

Curiosity piqued, Hayes couldn't resist delving further. "And what can you tell me about Captain Kane?" he asked.

"A dedicated and industrious man," Brooks replied, his gaze fixed on the ship's deck as if recalling memories.

"He climbed the ranks in the navy, eventually earning a place at the captain's table. He also pursued medical studies along the way, and now he's a man of both the sea and the healing arts."

Hayes's curiosity deepened. "Is Captain Kane from a well-known family, perhaps?" he probed, intrigued by the captain's multifaceted background.

Brooks shook his head. "Not at all. His father was a ship's captain on a trading vessel but was lost at sea when Kane was still a young lad."

Hayes couldn't hold back a question that had bothered him since his arrival. "If Kane is a doctor, why is my presence needed on board?"

Eager to start the task, Brooks responded with a touch of impatience. "He's no surgeon, I assure you. Now, let's focus on loading that pemmican. You can work with that burly seaman over there. His name is Goodfellow."

Goodfellow was an ordinary seaman with a broad chest, sturdy shoulders, and thick legs.

"Very well," Dr. Hayes agreed, walking purposefully. "I'll attend to it right away, Mr. Brooks."

"Remember to call me Mister Brooks, not sir!" Brooks called after him as Hayes went to work.

The crates and barrels made a gradual journey from the dock to the ship's deck, where they were meticulously lowered into the hold.

Hayes returned to Brooks with the completion of his task, ready to deliver his report.

In the backdrop, the ship's boats underwent the process of being securely lashed to the deck. Each boat proudly displayed a name painted on its bow: "Faith," "Hope," a brick-red lapstrake known as "Red Eric," and an innovative metal boat that, unlike the others, remained nameless.

"All the pemmican has been stowed per your instructions, Mr. Brooks," Hayes reported.

"Indeed," Brooks concurred, his gaze wandering over the gentle sway of the ships anchored in the harbor. "It's not often one encounters a ship's surgeon with hands capable of performing the labors of a sailor."

Hayes directed his attention toward the horizon, where the setting sun cast its golden hues across the expansive water.

"Life, it seems, is an endless sea of unexpected turns and new horizons," he mused. "Given the uncertainties this voyage may hold, naming our boats 'Faith' and 'Hope' feels fitting—almost poetic. But 'Red Eric'?"

He paused, a thoughtful furrow creasing his brow. "It's as if the final word from that New Testament phrase is missing."

Brooks interjected with a teasing glint in his eyes. "Indeed, and yet 'Charity' hasn't made its way onto this ship yet." Shifting back to a more severe tone, Hayes remarked, "I hope we won't have to rely on 'Hope' for anything other than exploring off-ship."

"That's the intention," Brooks affirmed. "Here's Petersen."

At that moment, the seasoned dog handler and sledge driver, Petersen, strode onto the gangplank, his arms laden with well-maintained dog harnesses. A native of American soil, Petersen had honed his skills running dog teams in the Canadian wilderness. His towering height, sharply defined features, and blond hair hinted at his Swedish lineage. Curious, Brooks gestured toward the harnesses and inquired, "Petersen, where might our canine companions be to fill those?"

With unwavering confidence, Petersen replied, "They'll join us en route," before vanishing below deck with his gear.

Hayes raised an eyebrow, doubt clear in his eyes. "I find it hard to believe how a wooden ship can..."

Before he could finish, Brooks interrupted, "Don't worry. The Advance is tougher than the men she carries. She's already proven herself in Arctic seas hauling iron. Mariah ain't gonna get her!"

Spotting Kane's tough-for-his-age and too-old-for-his-job, eighteen-years-old, freckled cabin boy, Tom Hickey, Brooks motioned him over and whispered, "Irish Tom, take this liquor and stow it securely in the captain's locker."

In the heart of the ship stood Blake, a compact man barely reaching five-foot-two. His hand-tailored, creased, and well-worn clothes mirrored the lines and stories etched into his weather-beaten face. Though not the most astute sailor on board, he was responsible for the boats. In a clumsy moment, he jammed his finger while trying to secure the metal boat single-handedly. Cursing under his breath, he lashed out with a boot, only to upset his balance further, sending a cascade of life jackets tumbling from his other arm.

Amid the flurry of activity on the ship, a few distinct figures stood out: Mr. Bonsall, the third officer, was imposing. His robust, square build and prominent jawline were a testament to a life facing challenges head-on. Alongside him worked Mr. McGary, with skin as worn as old leather and a face punctuated with a thick black, brushy mustache. His skills were invaluable as the ship's ice expert, navigator, and second officer. Then, there was Sven Ohlsen, a towering Swede renowned for his carpentry and boat design expertise.

Overseeing the bustling activity on deck, Ohlsen directed Johansson and Parker with a sharp eye and firm orders. The pair, known for their meticulous work as deckhands, expertly managed a towering pile of raw lumber. A few paces away, the slender figure of George Stevenson stood out. With every word he uttered, the distinct cadence of a British accent resonated in the air as he methodically loaded crates brimming with fresh cabbage.

Amidst this orchestrated chaos, George Whipple, Kane's trusted aide and the ship's steward, was engrossed in handling a particularly fragile piece of cargo. By his side, Pierre Schubert, the ship's nimble-fingered cook, flexed his tattoo-covered arms — each inked design hinting at a different adventure from distant lands. With shared precision, the two maneuvered a compact stove into place, securing it for the awaited voyage.

The dock's frenetic activity ebbed and flowed in sharp contrast—where piles of cargo once stood, now there were empty spaces; where the ship had been bare, it now brimmed with supplies. For Kane, every tick of the clock was a reminder that time was slipping too slowly. Yet he remained conflicted.

Was it wise to demand everything from the men now when the voyage would surely tax their limits later? He pondered if instilling strict discipline from the outset was the key or if it was more judicious to let them acclimate, gradually increasing their responsibilities. Each choice weighed heavily on him, a precursor to the leadership challenges that awaited.

Tension thickened when Sontag, the notoriously irritable scientist from the Smithsonian, arrived. Even by Swedish standards, his pale complexion betrayed years spent confined to a laboratory. He paced restlessly on the forecastle as the crew carefully loaded his precious instruments..

Leaning over the rail at the prow, Brooks, Ohlsen, Godfrey, and Hayes, their attention drawn to Ohlsen's freshly mounted, full-figured masthead. Its blue drapery and blushing pink cheeks seemed starkly out of place amidst the ship's ruggedness.

"She appears rather out of place here," Brooks mused, his gaze fixed on the delicate figure.

"Are you saying Augusta's too fragile a beauty for this sturdy vessel?" Hayes quipped.

From amidships, Sontag's voice carried, "He implies that she won't withstand the constant ice grazing."

Hayes looked up, uncertainty clouding his face. "And what about us?"

Ohlsen defended, "A few scrapes are part of her nature."

Brooks dismissed the worry with a wave, guiding the group back to the gangplank. "She's resilient."

Godfrey, the optimist, declared, "I've seen the Advance tackle ice much tougher than Augusta will face. She'll hold her own."

As they stepped aboard, Kane approached briskly, handing Brooks a sheet of paper. "Mr. Brooks, these are our sailing orders. Ensure every man is familiar with them before I address them individually."

Brooks raised an eyebrow, questioning, "Isn't that rather unconventional, sir?"

Kane's voice carried an edge, "We require unwavering dedication to the journey ahead."

Acknowledging the gravity of the situation, Brooks nodded, "Understood, sir," and promptly sought out the nearest crew member.

As Kane's instructions reverberated through the ship's wooden walls, Johansson and Parker, two crewmen, shouldered their sea bags and departed. Bonsall and Riley, stationed on the dock, exchanged curious glances.

"You can't fault them," Bonsall remarked. "The captain's transparency about our journey is certainly daunting."

In his distinct high-pitched voice, Riley admitted, "I might've missed his point, but if she's sailing, I'm going."

They redirected their attention to a weighty crate stamped "Fragile - Instruments," lifting it to carry aboard. Sontag, eyes shadowed with anxiety, observed their progress. And, in a misstep, Bonsall's sturdy grip slipped, causing the crate to crash onto the deck.

"You inept buffoons!" Sontag bellowed. "Can't you read? If you damaged anything inside, your voyage is over!"

Riley leaned close, whispering to Bonsall's ears, confessed, "Truth be told, I can't read." He raised his voice defiantly and challenged, "What's inside that's so precious? We've more gear aboard than a fleet would need."

Sontag's voice dripped with disdain. "Just stow it properly, vermin."

Tensions mounted as Riley bristled, ready to confront Sontag. But the situation was defused by the timely appearance of Kane and Brooks.

"Brooks, gather the crew," Kane ordered.

The ship's officers gathered, standing near but apart from the boisterous, ribbing crew. Suddenly, a brawl seemed imminent when Hickey threw a punch at Godfrey. However, it barely phased the larger man. After a quick push, Hickey was flat on his back. Brooks swiftly intervened, preventing further escalation by pinning Godfrey against the mast. Disoriented, Godfrey then stumbled and fell.

"Why the aggression, Hickey?" Kane inquired.

"He doubts your capability to lead," Hickey spat out.

Surveying his crew, Kane calmly responded, "On my own, his doubt might be founded. But with this team? He couldn't be more wrong."

Kane's icy stare met Godfrey's. "Stand, Godfrey. Either hold your peace for this voyage or leave this ship now. Which will it be?"

After a pause, Godfrey begrudgingly murmured, "Understood, sir," rejoining the crew. The group segregated naturally: officers on the elevated poop deck and crew below.

Before Kane addressed the men, Brooks confided, "With Godfrey, conflicts will linger."

Kane replied, "I'm counting on them finding their rhythm."

Brooks hesitated. "I hope you're right."

Kane turned to face the crew and spoke earnestly, "Men, we are about to embark on a mission of great importance and no small danger. We are sailing to the Arctic, searching for Sir John Franklin and his lost expedition.

Franklin and his men set sail in 1845 and have yet to return. Other expeditions have been searching for them, but they have not succeeded. We are determined to be the ones who finally bring them home, or at least discover their fate.

I don't need to remind you that the Arctic is dangerous. The weather is unpredictable, and the waters are treacherous. But we are a skilled and experienced crew, confident that we can succeed.

Our mission goes beyond finding Sir Franklin and his men; we seek to uncover the Arctic's many mysteries. We will chart unknown lands and gather valuable scientific knowledge.

I know each of you is ready for the challenge. As a band of brave, committed men, I am confident we shall succeed.

Now, I have one more thing to say. The first man to sight any sign of Sir Franklin's ship or men will receive a reward of a bottle of aged brandy."

The crew erupted in cheers.

As Kane concluded his speech, Sontag's voice cut through the silence, "And our departure?"

"At tomorrow's high tide," Kane affirmed. "Dismissed."

The crew cheered again.

The next morning, sails billowing under a warm May sun, the brig departed Annapolis. The northern horizon beckoned, urging them into uncharted waters as they ventured into the open sea. Kane's gaze was fixed on the cold, endless expanse before him, his mind racing with thoughts of the dangers that lay ahead. The crew, seasoned and resolute, moved with practiced precision, their voices harmonizing with the creaks and groans of the sturdy wooden vessel. Days turned into weeks as they navigated the treacherous Arctic waters, and a sense of anticipation filled the air. Though aware of the Arctic's perils, Kane's resolve to complete the mission remained firm.

IV. Fiskernaes Journey

Fiskernaes' view from the Governors' House

After a steady fifteen-day journey, on a cold, clear morning, the Advance dropped its anchor serenely in a quaint harbor adjacent to the village of Fiskernaes, a hamlet situated in southwestern Greenland on the Labrador Sea. Dominating the village's modest skyline was an imposing red and white frame mansion—its grandeur out of place amidst the humbler surroundings.

Upon disembarking, Kane, Brooks, Hayes, and McGary steered their metal boat toward the village dock. Despite their arrival, no one took notice, prompting the group to head directly to the mansion. A team of Esquimaux laborers was busy painting its porch. Kane watched them with unease, feeling as if they were observing him and his team closely. He approached a man who was overseeing the task.

"We're in search of the village superintendent," Kane inquired.

"He's at the pub," the man replied, momentarily distracted by a painter's error. "Not there! The railings, not the floor!" He exclaimed in exasperation. The Esquimaux painters shot him resentful glances, their tension intense. Sensing it was best to leave, Kane's group discreetly retreated and proceeded toward the village's solitary pub.

As they passed other residents of the remote settlement, Kane noticed that they all carried knives. He hoped it was out of necessity as fishermen and not an inclination toward violence.

Inside, the ambiance was reminiscent of a cozy English tavern tucked away in the northern English countryside. Bathed in soft illumination, the team approached a stout man with ruddy cheeks. He was conversing with an elder Esquimaux, his unlit pipe punctuating his gestures.

"Hitkoak, I've employed every able man available. Our funds are already stretched thin," he lamented.

The elder nodded, stood, and headed for the bar. Sensing an opening, Kane's party drew closer.

"You're the superintendent, I presume?" Kane queried.

"Indeed. Lassen is the name," the man replied, extending a hand.

Retrieving a letter from his coat, Kane said, "We bring an introduction from the Court of Denmark."

Lassen nonchalantly took the paper, absentmindedly rolling it into a tight cylinder. Without even a cursory glance, he used it to light his pipe from the candle on the table. Extinguishing the flame, he carelessly discarded the charred remains—a clear testament to the letter's irrelevance in this remote corner. Kane wondered why.

Kane and his crew settled around the table as the bartender placed four glasses before them. Lassen, the superintendent, filled each glass, offering a moment of camaraderie amid unfamiliar surroundings.

Kane began the introductions, his tone firm but amicable. "I am Captain Elisha Kane. Beside me are First Officer Henry Brooks, Second Officer James McGary, and our ship's surgeon, Dr. Robert Hayes. We're voyaging north aboard the brig, Advance."

Brooks swiftly got to the point, addressing their pressing needs. "We require fresh supplies, particularly food, and six Newfoundland sledge dogs."

Lassen raised an inquisitive eyebrow. "You're not on a whaling mission, then?"

"Certainly not," Kane clarified with conviction.

"Or a hunting venture, perhaps?" Lassen probed further.

Kane leaned in slightly, his voice carrying an air of solemnity. "We're in pursuit of the Franklin party that vanished four years ago. Ours is a mission of charity and discovery."

Understanding washed over Lassen's face. He took the charred paper, carefully smoothing its edges before returning it to Kane. "Your journey holds a different weight, then. The North is demanding. Even if you stock up on provisions, you'll be pressed for more. Do you have an Esquimaux hunter on board?"

Brooks responded quickly, with a hint of distaste in his tone, "We don't plan on relying on an Esquimaux for such crucial tasks."

The comment wasn't lost on the Esquimaux at the bar, who exchanged displeased glances. Lassen, unperturbed, added, "In these parts, the Esquimaux are every bit as cultured as... others." He paused, emptying his pipe and securing it in his pocket.

Sensing the strain, Kane said, "We could use an expert hunter—but one locally known who is not an Esquimaux?"

Lassen pondered momentarily, "There's only one—North of town if he's available. He goes by the name of Hans."

Rising with sudden purpose, Lassen beckoned them to follow. At the bar, an Esquimaux cast a cold glance at Brooks. Lassen set about arranging their supplies, his former leisure giving way to brisk efficiency. "We will have your needs met quickly. As for Hans—may fortune favor you."

Stepping outside, Lassen directed a pair of villagers, "Mr. Brooks, these fellows will aid you in gathering provisions and securing the dogs. Your captain and I will settle the finances later. For the rest of you, come along. Let's test the waters of fate."

Brooks stayed back as Lassen guided the rest up the village pathway. "Hans might prove a tad challenging in communication," Lassen mused. "His grasp of English is tenuous, and his southern dialect might be perplexing to the northern Esquimaux."

Kane, however, seemed undeterred, "No worries. A couple of our crewmembers acquired some rudimentary Esquimaux during prior northern expeditions. But rest assured, we don't plan on recruiting any northern Esquimaux for our mission."

They reached the village's outskirts, where the verdant hills beyond showcased patches of pristine snow near their peaks and nestled within deep crevices.

Lassen led them to a modest dwelling and rapped at the door. From behind an upturned kayak stepped a tall, broad-shouldered young Esquimaux, his sudden appearance giving the crew pause. A moment later, the door opened to an elderly woman, her face deeply lined, her small frame diminished beside the young man. In her silence, it was plain he held the household's lead.

Hans Christian

Though but nineteen, he looked older. For an Esquimaux, his height was remarkable—nearly six feet. Broad shoulders and sinewed arms told of labor and strength. He wore a fox-skin Kapetah, and at his neck hung a whale-tooth pendant carved in the shape of a polar bear. He greeted Lassen warmly, while the old woman kept her silent watch..

"Captain, meet Hans," Lassen introduced.

Kane blurted, "but, he's an Esquimaux." Hans raised an eyebrow.

"And, the best you will find in these parts," Lassen said. "He is what you'll need."

Hans looked quizzically at Kane, "Who you?"

"Captain of the Advance," Kane replied.

Hans' puzzled gaze persisted. "Who you?" he pressed.

"The leader of the ship in the harbor," Kane simplified.

A hint of amusement flashed in Hans' eyes. Lassen intervened, "He's Doctor Kane. Hans here is unparalleled with spears."

With a challenging grin, Hans asked, "You wish to see?"

Kane nodded. In a fluid motion, Hans grabbed a spear resting against the house and thrust it, piercing a distant barrel through and through.

"Remarkable," Kane remarked, "but our prey might not be standing still."

"Then see his hand with the javelin," Lassen urged.

As Hans reached for a shorter javelin, Lassen surreptitiously fetched a driftwood piece. He hurled it skyward, and with impeccable precision, Hans intercepted it mid-flight with the spear.

"He's also adept at finding and tracking seals," Lassen mentioned.

"We journey north for several months, perhaps a year. Would you join us, Hans?" Kane inquired.

"If mother is cared for, I ask two dollars monthly," Hans negotiated.

"Done," Kane agreed. "We'll leave barrels of provisions for her. Mr. Lassen, would you oversee her well-being while Hans is away? We'll compensate upon our return."

"We can arrange an advance now and finalize any discrepancies upon your return," Lassen suggested.

Hans, still processing, wondered, "Why venture north?"

"To search for missing ships and men and explore unknown terrains. We aim to chart lands, document climates, and gather unique samples," Kane explained.

"I help in searches and hunting," Hans clarified.

"That suffices," Kane responded. "Join us aboard the Advance in two hours."

Hans nodded, "I come now."

Sensing the mission's urgency, Lassen asked, "Would you honor us with your presence for dinner this evening?"

Kane, ever the pragmatist, replied, "Our brief summer compels us to utilize every moment. We have much to do – provisioning, organizing, and finalizing accounts. Perhaps on our return voyage?"

Lassen nodded, "If fates allow."

Within the hour, they were back at sea. The coastline was barren and rocky, and as the sea began to rise, occasional icebergs came into view.

They sailed on choppy seas dotted with smaller icebergs for weeks. Every so often, the crew would stare out at the infinite icy horizon, pondering the mysteries it hid.

Then, a fierce gale assailed them. The tumultuous waves battered the ship, sending the six tethered Newfoundland dogs skidding back and forth across the deck.

Seeking shelter, the brig anchored in a secluded cove near Lichtenfels Sound, a stark expanse home to only a few huts and their inhabitants.

From the ship, the crew gazed at the majestic Sukkertop Mountain with its jagged peak rising three thousand feet, defying the ocean's depths below. A rugged gorge sprawled beneath the mountain; its contours so intricate that man-made stairways were needed to connect the scattered clusters of huts. These fragile dwellings clung to the rocks, appearing as nature's whimsical creations. The homes stood isolated at high tide, turning into fleeting islands amidst the vastness.

As the storm eased, Brooks and Petersen, guided by Hans, went ashore, trading ironware like knives for the Indigenous Esquimaux tools and attire — including deer-skin garments and seal-skin shoes. Their coastal trek led them through the sparse settlements, where Petersen traded and acquired sledges and more dogs for their expedition.

Greenland Sledges

In the weeks that followed, Kane and his crew pushed a thousand miles farther north—far as from New York to Chicago. They battled the sea's shifting moods, weathered storms, and steered clear of looming icebergs. Now they stood at the edge of the known world. Beyond lay only the unknown: solitude, mutual dependence, and the constant shadow of danger.

Their last touchpoint with civilization was in Upernavik. Here, the icy grip of the Arctic held the shoreline hostage, with baby icebergs acting as sentinels amidst the cold waves. Plumes of smoke whispered tales of life from within the distant igloos, spiraling into the bleak sky. These icy domes stood resilient, the sole guardians against the Arctic's ferocity. As if to mock the ship, dovekies — the region's tuxedoed seabirds — swirled around its rigging, appearing like plump, monochrome specters.

Returning to the ship after a bartering visit ashore, Petersen, Baker, and Whipple faced the herculean task of wrangling a lively pack of Huskies onto the deck. Meanwhile, the resident Newfoundland dogs, more seasoned, watched their every move with a blend of curiosity and skepticism. The youthful and exuberant Huskies treated the deck as their playground, their snouts probing and sniffing, instigating playful tussles to establish dominance in their newfound territory.

A cold unease crept over the crew as the Advance departed, and Upernavik faded into the horizon. It wasn't the chill of the Arctic wind but the dawning realization that they were venturing into a vast unknown. From here on, it would be a journey of sheer self-reliance, navigating unknown and uncharted waters toward uncertain destinations. A single oversight or miscalculation could consign them to the icy abyss forever.

V. Beyond Upernavik

A week later, the ship lay stagnant in an expansive stillness. Aboard Hope and Faith, the ship's two sturdy boats, four men in each, rowed strenuously, carving a path between looming icebergs that stood sentinel in this icy realm. The familiar coast had diminished to a distant outline, and the ominous silhouette of dark clouds cast a grim tableau ahead.

"The in-shore route's no longer an option," remarked Brooks, his breath visible in the cold.

Kane, squinting towards the horizon, replied, "Turn her westward. The water-sky to the north will guide us." A chilling reflection painted the clouds above, hinting at the water beneath.

Brooks scanned the icy maze, saying, "We're surrounded. Call McGary to the deck."

At this latitude, the concept of day and night was losing its traditional meaning. Summer's endless daylight was turning to winter's perpetual darkness, with interludes of fleeting nights or days. As the Advance made its way deeper into the Arctic, the stretch of daylight dwindled, and the shroud of night grew longer.

With night just beginning its descent, Kane retired below deck, leaving the helm in Whipple's competent grasp, whose sturdy forearms and robust legs gave testament to his countless battles with the sea.

An hour later, Whipple yelled. "Call the captain! The ice paths are sealing up!" Morton, busy with the lines, sprinted below.

Moments later, Kane emerged, swiftly gauging their predicament. Orders flew from his lips as Blake, Baker, Godfrey, Stevenson, Petersen, and Shubert sprang into coordinated chaos: sails adjusted, lines secured, and dogs tethered. From the bow, McGary, eyes sharp from his ice watch, hurriedly reported, "The wind's pushing the ice in on us."

"To the leeward of that iceberg!" Kane ordered, pointing decisively. "Blake, Baker, ready ice anchors!"

The ship glided slowly, shadowed by a colossal iceberg that loomed taller than its mast and stretched beyond both the ship's width and length. Despite repeated attempts, Blake and Baker struggled to secure an ice anchor, resembling a grappling hook, into the behemoth's side. Observing their efforts in vain, Kane decided on a change in tactics.

"Mr. Brooks, furl the rest of the sails," Kane yelled. "The wind is slackening. Bonsall, take Godfrey, Blake, and Baker and launch the red boat. Row to that large berg and make fast a line." As he said that, the winds died down.

In the dead calm of midnight, Bonsall and his men rowed the Red Eric toward the berg, forcing their way for hours through a thick drift of slush, ice lumps, and small floes. The berg's high, angular sides offered little purchase, and securing a line proved maddeningly difficult. Crewmen took turns at the task, each near spent.

After many attempts, Godfrey finally got a line anchored. The boat crew then battled their way back to the ship. After other crewmen helped them reload and secure the red boat to the deck, the crew slumped down on the deck, exhausted from exertion and mental strain. With the line anchored, other crew members hauled the brig up next to the berg and tied her tight. The side of the berg towered over the ship, standing at least thirty feet above the top of the mainmast.

With the brig secured by the berg, Kane addressed the crew, most of them cold, some wet, and all tired beyond exhaustion, as they filed below.

"Your hard work has gotten us a secure anchorage," Kane said. "Hot food and well-earned rest wait below."

Kane and Brooks remained topside to consider their next actions.

"Come morning, we'll need to work out of this pack ice," Brooks said.

"Post a night watch for changes in winds or currents," Kane said. "That offshore gale could move back our way. We're at least twenty miles from open. . ." Interrupted in mid-sentence, Kane and Brooks saw and felt walnut-sized ice fragments hitting the water and the deck of the ship like rain. At the same time, a loud crackling sound from above startled them into realization. Kane jumped for an ax and chopped through the line holding the ship to the berg.

"Call the crew on deck!" he shouted.

Brooks leapt to the hatch and hollered below.

"All hands on deck! All hands on deck!"

"Push off!" Kane shouted as men appeared on deck and jumped into action. "We need to move away from the berg, now!"

Others rushed onto the deck. Brooks directed the first men to arrive to start pushing the ship away with poles. But given the current and the ship's weight, their efforts seemed futile. Kane, alongside Godfrey, grabbed a pole. With their combined strength, the ship began to inch away. Just as they cleared twenty feet, the face of the berg collapsed in a cascade of ice between the brig and the ship, creating resounding booms akin to artillery fire. The brig was jostled away from the berg, with blocks of ice and pads shifting rapidly around them. At last, the ship found its stability in the now-calm sea.

"I suppose fastening to the berg was not such a good idea," Kane said to Brooks.

Brooks gave a wry smile. "Unfortunately, I think we can't stay here either."

It took the crew hours of hard labor to work the ship free and thread her through the surrounding ice.

The following morning, shrouded by a thick fog, the ship lay tethered in the shadow of a monolithic iceberg drifting lazily on the waves. Six weary men, their faces etched with fatigue, leaned heavily against the gunwale.

"Captain, is there not a harbor where we might find respite?" Hayes ventured, his voice betraying a mix of hope and desperation.

"There are no reliable charts for these waters," Kane replied. "Ours show only the larger islands and indistinct shorelines. We must take what shelter we can."

Turning his gaze to the gray expanse, Kane addressed his crew with a reassuring firmness, "Our journey has only just begun, men. This berg should protect us for now."

Breathless from dashing from the foredeck, Riley interrupted, "Captain! Two bears spotted on firm ice, about half a mile northward."

Kane's eyes lit up with a new purpose. "Petersen, take Hans and Wilson in the Red. Go after them," he commanded, "I'll be right behind with Morton in the Hope. Bear meat will do us good. Brooks, ensure the ship doesn't stray too far from our boats. We don't want to get separated."

An hour later, the Advance was nestled among floating ice sheets in the waning pallid light, bordering a vast plateau of solid ice. Using long poles, the men steered their boats along the icy edge, their gaze fixed on the silhouette of Hans. Armed solely with his spear, he appeared as a lone hunter, tracking the elusive paths of polar bears across the solid ice.

Morton, peering into the encroaching mist, whispered, "There! Just ahead."

Struggling to discern, Kane asked, "Where?"

Petersen, pointing, advised, "Look closely. Their shapes are merging with the fog."

Wilson's voice cut through the cold. "Hans—after them!"

With unwavering resolve, Hans dashed forward, soon enveloped by the thickening mist.

Time seemed to stand still as the men, anchored in their boats amongst the drifting floes, waited anxiously for Hans's return. Hans's figure gradually took shape, approaching them like a specter emerging from the mists. Once he returned, he declared, "The tracks no more."

Peering ahead, Kane noticed open water. At first, it was a faint sight; however, as the fog dissipated, Kane could see an expanse of open water just beyond a massive iceberg.

"Open water!" Kane exclaimed. "Hurry, back to the brig."

"Nanook led us here," Hans remarked, stepping into the red boat.

Kane gave him a doubtful look.

As the crew members hoisted themselves onto the deck, fatigue evident in their every move, Petersen reported to Brooks, "There's a stretch of open water, or perhaps a sizable lead, roughly a mile ahead."

"And the bears?" Brooks asked, a hint of anticipation in his voice.

"They were only but shadows," Kane added. "Gather the men."

The vast icefields compromised their northern progress, sapping precious time with each passing day. Entrapped by shifting ice, the brig took refuge by anchoring to a colossal iceberg, following in the wake of the dark waters it disturbed.

VI. Northern Waters

Sheets of floating ice closed in from all sides. Just after midnight, the Advance managed to break free from the icy clutches and ventured into the boundless open waters of the Arctic Ocean, its glistening expanse beckoning them northward.

On the bridge, Whipple turned to Kane, breaking the contemplative silence. "It seems we've finally made it through."

Kane, measured in his response, said, "For now."

"Shall we steer due north?"

Kane nodded in agreement. "Once you spot Hakluyt Island, alert the watch. It represents the furthest point on our charts. Beyond that, we chart our own course."

Brooks emerged from the shadows, advancing towards them. Kane issued a command, "Brooks, double the watch. Keep a sharp eye for looming icebergs. After that, rest. I'll be in my cabin should you need me."

By daybreak, a raging blizzard had taken hold, its blinding fury blanketing everything as the Advance grappled with the mighty waves. On the deck, shielded by a stowed lifeboat, Godfrey and Riley, wrapped in heavy attire, methodically sewed blanket bags, and readied tools for forthcoming searches. Above, Ohlsen, with a steadfast grip on the helm, maintained an unwavering focus on the treacherous sea before him. The rest of the deck lay hauntingly deserted.

"I used to sew sails with my father," Godfrey reminisced, fingers moving expertly. "He'd chuckle seeing me like this."

"He was a sailor?" Riley inquired.

A disdainful look crossed Godfrey's face. "He was a Captain, not some mere seaman."

Oblivious to the sting in Godfrey's words, Riley pressed on, "Where's he now? Why aren't you serving under his command?

A flicker of sorrow crossed Godfrey's eyes. "He's gone. He had dreams of seeing me become a captain. When I missed my chance, the weight of his disappointment might've been his undoing."

Riley paused, then shared, "My father sailed on countless vessels."

Godfrey stared into the white fury beyond the rail. "From here on, every step is uncharted. I doubt any soul on Earth would wish our lot."

Riley leaned in, voice low. "We ought to hide a few provisions— a safeguard."

Godfrey's brow rose. "Unless you speak of mutiny, a few stashed rations will serve no one"

"Only testing your mettle," Riley said with a sly grin.

A shadow crossed Godfrey's face, anger simmering in his eyes. "Try that again, and you won't like the outcome."

The unmistakable anger between them erupted. In a sudden move, Godfrey lunged forward, his hand tightening around Riley's throat and lifting him slightly off the ground. Gagging for breath, Riley managed to break free, stumbling backward. He coughed violently, the red hue of his face slowly retreating. "I was merely suggesting we keep some extra food aside in case supplies run short," he rasped out.

Godfrey, his anger subsiding, looked at him with disdain and understanding. "A few extra rations in this icy wasteland won't make much difference. But perhaps we should stash some in case our supplies run low or conditions worsen."

Riley nodded, rubbing his sore neck. "I hope we're not on another doomed voyage."

On the foredeck, Kane and McGary scanned the horizon. A distant glint of ice captured their attention, standing as a warning. "Ice ahead?" Kane asked, seeking confirmation.

McGary nodded solemnly. "The northern wind carries more than just a chill."

After heading below deck, Riley and Godfrey swiftly stowed their work items. When they returned topside, the ship was a hive of activity. Kane shouted instructions to Ohlsen at the helm, while Blake and Brooks prepared for an expedition.

"Speed is of the essence; that storm's drawing near," Kane said tersely. "We need to set up a supply cache on that island before it hits, giving us a safety net for the return journey."

Blake, murmuring to himself, continued with his duties.

Pemmican

An hour later, onshore, the crew labored without pause, utilizing the natural landscape to construct a cairn shielding their cache. The tension in the air was thick. Dr. Hayes scanned the expansive wilderness, feeling the ever-present danger around them.

Hans noticed Hayes's apprehensive expression.

Seeing their exchange, Kane said reassuringly, "This cairn isn't meant to safeguard our cache from the Esquimaux. It's primarily to ward off curious polar bears. The rocks and frozen layers should suffice.

Hayes's eyes flitted across the desolate landscape, with every shadow causing his heart to skip. He was, however, unprepared for Shubert's sudden scream that shattered the Arctic stillness. Shubert had taken a tumble down an embankment.

His cry wasn't just due to the fall but from the shock of finding himself precariously close to ancient skeletal remains. A bone lay in his grasp, and the grim sight wrenched another scream that echoed against the icy cliffs.

The skeleton was nestled against the embankment, knees drawn up to its chest as though it had sought refuge from the relentless winds in its last moments. It appeared to be in silent contemplation of the expansive sea ahead. Tattered remnants of what once were animal skins clung loosely to its frame. A tangible unease swept over the crew, prompting many to step back. Still reeling from the shock, Shubert took refuge just beyond the ridge.

Hans and the ever-curious Dr. Hayes, however, approached with caution, finding additional bones scattered nearby.

"What could have transpired here?" Shubert called out, his face cautiously peering over the ridge. "Is this the grim aftermath of an attack? Could this be one of Franklin's crew?"

Hayes confirmed, "This isn't one of Franklin's men. In addition to this lone Inuk, the surrounding bones likely belong to his prey—possibly narwhal, walrus, or even a few foxes."

"Could he have taken his own life?" Shubert wondered aloud.

Hayes shook his head. "There's no indication of suicide. He chose this spot, facing the sea, to meet his end. His motives remain a mystery—perhaps old age. He had sustenance, suggesting it wasn't a hasty decision."

"Among the Inuit, life and death are intertwined with the unpredictability of nature," Kane interjected. "Our main concern is the cairn. Let's complete that."

Hans watched as Hayes set the artifacts around the bones, then covered them with stones..

"Shall we raise our cairn on that rise?" Hayes asked, pointing toward it.

Kane surveyed the surroundings. "While the windbreak here is beneficial, we won't mark this as a tribute to the Inuk. We'll place ours there." He gestured to a spot a short distance to the east.

With determination, they erected the cairn, completing it with a stone pyramid at its peak. Kane placed a note inside a protective canister and nestled it among the topmost stones as a final addition. He retrieved a small American flag from his coat and firmly secured it at the cairn's pinnacle.

"This will serve as our landmark for anyone who travels this path," Kane declared. "May the heavens be merciful to Sir Franklin and his crew. And if fate decides that we do not pass this way again, may that same mercy apply to us."

A few days later, the horizon darkened ominously as the nights stretched on. Advance's journey had yet to bring her as far northward as Kane had hoped, and the worsening conditions reflected their troubled course.

VII. Arctic Challenges

The brig lay trapped in an open channel, hemmed by two icebergs. Above, the sky held no trace of Dovekies, and the sea struck hard against the hull. The cold bit into the men's faces, icing their beards, while the wind's shriek cut through them. Brooks and Whipple leaned close to speak, their white-knuckled hands gripping the wheel though the ship lay at anchor.

"This is more than a storm; it's a raging fury," Brooks yelled. "Our moorings should hold, but lash yourself to the helm in case they don't." Whipple tied himself in while Brooks held the wheel.

Inside the cabin, under the stern gaze of Sir Franklin from a framed newspaper clipping, Kane meticulously updated his log, his words an effort to document the chaos outside: "The hurricane's wrath is turning the ice into living demons." He was interrupted by a loud, resonant "twang," like a giant bowstring being released, signaling the ominous snap of a hawser. Before he could fully react, Stevenson's frantic voice from above confirmed his fears.

"The six-inch hawser's gone!" Stevenson hollered breathlessly.

No sooner had he spoken than two more, higher-pitched twangs echoed – the unmistakable sound of the whale lines giving way.

Wasting no time, Kane scrambled onto the deck, fighting to the helm. "Report!" he demanded.

"Our moorings, both fore and aft, are gone!" Brooks cried out. "One manila line remains, but it's fraying fast."

McGary, battling against the fierce winds, yelled, "Captain, we can't hold on! We can't free the line; if we cut it, we're adrift."

Amidst the chaos, a haunting sound enveloped the ship. Blake, face drained of color, screamed, "Eolian chant! We're cursed!"

Nearby, Riley, eyes wide with terror, dashed for the safety below. "The death song!" he howled.

In a determined bid to quell the rising panic, Kane shouted above the din, "It's just the wind's lament through our rigging. Hold fast, men!"

But the universe had other plans. Under the strain, the manila line began to snap, strand by strand, each break sounding like the crack of a gun. When the final tether snapped, the ship was left to the mercy of the raging ice and sea, tossed about in the storm's frenzy. Waves surged over them, their icy embrace threatening to pull them under. Whipple, his every muscle straining, battled with the wheel.

"Hold it steady, Whipple! Keep steering us through this drifting maze!" Kane bellowed, rallying his crew amidst nature's fury.

The tempest raged, each gust threatening to throw the brig into the ice's lethal embrace.

"Godfrey, Ohlsen! Reef the topsails immediately!" Brooks' voice sliced through the howling gale. Without hesitation, the two men, risking their lives, ascended the rope ladder to the crow's nest, navigating deftly through the rigging to tame the unruly sailcloth.

"Brooks, tie yourself starboard!" Kane's voice was urgent. "McGary, you too, up front! I've got port."

Whipple wrestled with the helm; every muscle strained as the ship's bow grated against encroaching ice. "Augusta's nose-first into the storm!" he bellowed, fighting for a grip against the ship's relentless sway.

Kane's gaze sharpened at the looming ice masses. 'Petersen, Bonsall! Deploy the heavy anchor! We need it to slow us down to navigate through that ice."

Both men wrestled with the anchor; every muscle strained, and it dropped with a loud clatter. The anchor's drag was sufficient, but it was excessive. The ice was now primarily targeting the stern. Kane's face paled as he realized the situation. "Cut the anchor!"

Amid the chaos, Petersen risked his life, securing a beam to the anchor chain in the hope of retrieving it later. As the anchor plunged into the sea, its chain whipped out, ensnaring his leg, and violently dragging him toward the ship's edge. In a desperate move, Bonsall lunged forward, his fingers clamping onto Petersen's ankles and freeing him from the chain's grasp, averting a potential watery tragedy.

With the anchor gone, the ship was ruthlessly propelled into the approaching ice mountains. When a colossal ice chunk crashed onto the deck, Brooks executed a life-saving dive, narrowly avoiding being crushed. Torrents of water swept one of the Newfoundland dogs overboard, transforming the deck into an ice-slick battlefield.

Tumbling along the icy deck, McGary finally managed to reach Kane.

"There—a passage between those bergs!" McGary cried, then froze. "No—ice is closing in. We'll be trapped!"

Kane ordered Whipple hard to port, but the converging walls gave no quarter. The crew's efforts to fend them off failed. A sudden jolt hurled Blake against the doghouse, where he lay still.

The advancing berg seemed like salvation, and McGary secured it with an ice-anchor. The ship trailed the iceberg, but their path grew perilously narrow.

"Brace the yards!" Kane commanded Ohlsen and Godfrey. "Baker, Bonsall! Secure the starboard boat."

In the scramble, Bonsall lost his footing and slid toward the rail. Baker lunged, seizing his collar. The weight dragged them both, but Baker held fast, stopping their slide.

As they passed the unconscious Blake, they seized him by the collar and dragged him to safety below deck. The ship groaned, wood splintering and metal shearing as they escaped. Their jib boom wasn't so fortunate, torn away by the remorseless ice.

The storm's fury seemed endless, each moment filled with heart-stopping pressure and the ever-present threat of the unforgiving Arctic grasp.

"There—open water! A cove beyond the point!" McGary shouted through the wind.

Kane's voice, tinged with hope, cut through the bluster. "Mr. Whipple, make for that cove!"

Whipple glanced at the massive iceberg leading them. "If our captor allows our escape, sir," he responded, a note of irony tinged with worry.

The towed ship followed the iceberg's lead, precariously skirting the point's edge. Blake, still recovering, staggered onto the deck, his presence a testament to the crew's resilience. Eyes widened as the iceberg's fate became apparent. It grounded, shuddering and tilting precariously over the ship.

Kane's shout carried urgency. "Mr. Ohlsen—cut us loose! We must swing into that cove. Mr. Whipple, make for the shore, but beware of the tidal surge!"

Ohlsen swung the ax, severing the tether, and the ship broke free. It wheeled around the point, edging toward the cove's shelter—only for the tide to drop with startling speed. The hull struck bottom and listed sharply. Boats crashed, booms swung, dogs scrambled, and men stumbled as barrels and gear slid across the deck, which had become a perilous slope. Then a ridge of shore ice caught the ship, jarring her but stopping the slide. Damaged yet spared, she righted slowly and drifted into the cove, where the crew found brief refuge.

Kane, as though he had carried the world's weight, patted Whipple's back and approached Brooks. "Anchor us securely. I'll stand watch. Rest, Mr. Brooks. We'll need every ounce of your strength tomorrow."

"Aye, Captain," Brooks acknowledged, weariness evident in his tone.

Hours later, muscles aching, and mind fogged with fatigue, Kane trudged to his cabin, hoping for sanctuary. Instead, he was met with chaos—his possessions submerged in salty water. Clearing his soaked desk, he retrieved the ship's log, determined to document the ordeal. He detailed the ship's state and the diminishing prospects of their mission. However, he left his deepest fears unrecorded—the growing possibility that their search for Franklin might evolve into a desperate struggle for survival against the impending winter.

VIII. Winter Shelter

A few days later, amidst blowing snow, some of the "Advance" crew on the shore towed the brig along the ice. Their effort was reminiscent of mules pulling a laden barge along the Erie Canal. With muscles bulging, they hauled with the raw strength of their shoulders, aided by rue-raddies – rugged leather harnesses – anchored to the ship with durable whale lines. They were making progress when Kane's voice brought them to a sudden stop.

"Hold up!" Kane shouted from the helm of the "Advance."

From the icy shore, Brooks's voice carried clear against the wind, "Everybody stop!"

Without missing a beat, Kane ordered, "Wilson, Petersen, Bonsall—get aboard!"

Fighting the gale, the three clambered up, faces raw and beards crusted with frost.

Kane, sensing they brought valuable information, asked, "Report?"

Bonsall, his voice edged with cold, replied, "Captain, between that distant island and our position, there's potential shelter. The water's dark shade suggests depth and looks protected from the prevailing winds." He gestured despite the numbing cold gripping his fingers.

Kane sought McGary's expertise to grasp the gravity of their situation, especially with the looming winter. "McGary, your thoughts?"

With his discerning eyes scanning the area, McGary pulled a small brass telescope from his coat for a closer look. "It's promising, Captain. Perhaps the best shelter we've sighted."

With the crew's safety paramount in his mind, Kane decided. "Brooks, a new tactic. We'll tow the "Advance" there, using our boats. Let's get to that sanctuary."

The crew moved at once, snow swirling about them. The smaller boats—Hope and Faith—were quickly launched and secured to the Advance. Men passed between ship and boats, their practiced coordination the key to working in such waters.

By the following night, the Advance nestled on the island's leeward side, safely tucked halfway between its rocky embrace and the mainland, anchored in waters sixty feet deep. In the dim glow of lanterns below deck, voices murmured. Several crewmen, Brooks among them, huddled at the mess table. Godfrey and a few others lingered nearby. An air of relaxation prevailed.

"The new ice is six inches thick, and it drops to twenty-five degrees each night," McGary warned. "Old ice is denser and tougher."

Brooks replied, "A strong wind could still free us. We need to be farther north for our mission."

Petersen added, "This place will wear on us and our dogs. We should head south now, then return north in the spring."

Agreement buzzed amongst the crew. Sontag and Hans observed the exchange silently.

"We need to keep moving north," Brooks insisted. "Going back now will only cost us time in the spring."

Godfrey, clearly irritated, confronted Brooks. "What makes you so smart, Brooks? Do you know how bad the ice might get?"

Sensing the escalating conflict, Brooks met Godfrey's gaze, steeling himself for the confrontation ahead.

"Hah!" Brooks shot back, defiance evident in his tone. "You wouldn't know the first thing about it, Godfrey."

Without warning, Godfrey's restraint snapped. He lunged at Brooks, landing a powerful punch on his jaw. The force sent Brooks reeling into a cupboard. Another man might've been knocked out, but Brooks wasn't so easily defeated. Blood on his lips and a fierce determination in his eyes, he responded with a solid blow to Godfrey's cheek. The two men clashed fiercely, their punches becoming more desperate as exhaustion quickly took over. The chaotic scene continued until McGary and Bonsall stepped in, doing their best to separate the combatants.

Amid the commotion, Godfrey, his pride stinging, made a move to strike McGary. But McGary stood his ground, locking eyes with him and warning in an icy tone, "Think twice about that, laddie."

Kane stepped in, voice cutting through the din. "Godfrey, you've crossed the line. A ship cannot stand disorder." He motioned to Bonsall and Ohlsen. "Confine him in the store-room until I give word."

Godfrey resisted, yelling back, "Brooks pushed me to it!"

Kane's gaze stayed cold. "Words, man—answer with words, not blows."

The crew shifted uncomfortably, the weight of the altercation laying heavy in the atmosphere.

Kane addressed the remaining crew, "Our mission stands. This bay will serve as our winter quarters. Anyone who thinks otherwise best resign themselves to my command."

The following morning brought the cold, biting air and a need for resolution. On the deck, Kane, flanked by Hans, Bonsall, and Petersen, addressed the crew and a subdued Godfrey.

"For your reckless actions, Godfrey, you'll be on Firehole duty once the ice thickens. Bonsall, Petersen, oversee his work."

Nodding, Godfrey seemed resigned to his fate, the earlier fire in his eyes now a mere ember.

With a nod to Brooks, Kane added, "Prep the supplies for McGary. We're dispatching a team northward to establish caches for our spring trek."

Hans interjected with a puzzled look, "Why caches?"

"To stock pemmican and fuel in the areas we'll be exploring, ensuring we have them on hand if or when needed," Kane explained.

Hans, searching Kane's eyes, mused aloud, "There are many ways to proceed."

Kane, lost in thoughts of the upcoming expedition, signaled Whipple. "We anchor here until the team returns."

Overhearing their conversation, McGary chimed in, "Preparing for an outing, Captain?"

"Indeed," Kane replied. "We must learn how far north Franklin went—perhaps as far as the Pole. There are miles yet to cover."

"We depart at first light then," McGary said, determined.

Sheltered by their small island, the brig lay fast in waters hardening to ice beneath the biting cold.

IX. Abyss of Rats

From the deck, Kane and Brooks watched the depot party—McGary, Bonsall, Baker, Whipple, Godfrey, Stevenson—progressing northward, tasked with erecting two cairns as far into the vastness as possible, their silhouettes receding against the frozen shore.

"This weather is more merciless than anticipated," voiced Kane, his gaze veiled in shadows. "We are not even in the dead of winter. Nature could obliterate us in short order."

"The looming perpetual dark and relentless ice will limit our searches," commented Brooks.

A subtle yet noticeable disturbance began behind Brooks. Kane's attention immediately zeroed in on it. "What's the crew up to?" he asked, eyebrows furrowing.

"The rats have pushed them to the edge," Brooks replied. "They're fumigating the quarters using brimstone, burnt leather, and arsenic. They've sealed every entrance, and Dr. Hayes has lit the stoves below."

Suddenly, chaos erupted on deck. Riley emerged, gasping for air. Kane and Brooks rushed to the scene.

"What's going on?" Kane demanded.

"Pierre went below with Riley and hasn't come back," Morton reported, casting a concerned look toward the smoke-filled entrance.

"And Dr. Hayes?" Kane pressed.

Morton pointed, "He's over there," indicating Dr. Hayes, who stood a short distance away.

Rushing down the ladder into the dense smoke below deck, Kane found Pierre slumped against a bulkhead. Morton, Ohlsen, and Wilson came right behind Kane. Together, they dragged Pierre up the ladder. Once topside, the fresh air enveloped them as Kane and Morton supported the weakened Pierre.

"The vapors might've taken out a few rats," Kane said, fixing the crew with a stern gaze, "but a fire could kill us all. We'll live with the rats if we must. From now on—fires only in the stove."

The weary sun cast its final light over the ice, its rays dimming as thick snow began to fall, blanketing the ship. On the frost-covered deck, Kane and Dr. Hayes exchanged tense words, their breaths visible in the frigid air, momentarily visible before being swallowed by the falling snow. Around them, the ice had set hard, forming a firm track for men and sledges along the shore.

"Your extreme measures scarcely made a dent in the rat population," Kane remarked, a hint of annoyance in his tone.

"We discovered twenty-eight lifeless bodies over the fortnight, all appearing well-nourished," retorted Hayes.

"Regrettably, the majority seem to have survived."

Interrupting their exchange, Petersen sprinted up the gangway, urgency painted across his features.

"Captain—quick!" he implored. "The nursing bitch is acting strangely."

With growing concern, they quickly descended to the icy floor where the dogs were tethered. A female husky, allowed to roam freely because of her maternal status, moved with a strange, erratic shuffle.

"I fear it might be hydrophobia," Kane said, his voice filled with worry.

"That seems unlikely," Hayes countered. "Aren't such cases rare this far north? We haven't seen any Arctic foxes or other wildlife since we arrived."

"Perhaps the rats," suggested Hayes.

Suddenly, the distressed dog lunged at Hans, veering toward Petersen before collapsing at his feet, her jaws frothy with foam. A sense of dread settled over the group as Hayes spoke to Petersen.

"She's a danger to the pack. We have no choice but to put her and her offspring down," Hayes said, hushed and heavy.

Petersen's face fell. After a moment, he drew his pistol, the metal cold in his hand, and carried out the grim task.

That evening, as the depot party returned, the chill of the outside world seemed to cling to them. They quickly gathered around the stove, enveloped in the comforting sounds of crackling wood and flickering flames. Wilson's fingers glided over his guitar, filling the space with spirited sea shanties that lifted the spirits of the gathered men.

"I take it there was no trace of Franklin?" Hayes asked, his voice tinged with both hope and concern.

"None," McGary replied tersely, the weight of his words heavy.

"And what of the Esquimaux?" Kane pressed, his eyes searching.

"No," McGary responded, concern shadowing his expression. "But encountering them is only a matter of time. We've set up three caches, hoping they stay untouched."

Bonsall chimed in, his voice somber, "In the ninety miles we covered, we found no better winter harbor for our ship than here."

His voice echoing the weight of their reality, McGary pronounced, "The 'eternal night' begins now."

The room grew heavy with the weight of his words, a collective acknowledgment of the looming darkness and piercing cold ahead, and beneath it all, unvoiced fears and hopes still clung.

Weeks into the unyielding darkness, Kane, nearly swallowed by shadows, diligently recorded his customary measurements on deck. The dim glow from the swaying lanterns on the spar-deck, dancing gently in the brisk wind, only faintly outlined his silhouette against the engulfing black. Unhooking one of the lanterns, Kane illuminated the ship's clock, its hands pointing to 12 on the 24-hour dial. Just then, McGary emerged from the depths of the Advance.

"It's time for our noon meal," he remarked, his voice punctuating the silence and hinting at a more profound question, "How much longer until we see daylight again?"

"In ninety days, we'll see the first hint of light, and in a hundred and forty, the sun will shine on us again," Kane replied softly.

As he spoke, McGary pulled out a fragment of blue cloth adorned with tiny red roses and white trim from beneath his coat.

Observing the condensation on his thermometer, Kane remarked, "My breath frosts the glass. It probably reads minus twenty-three. May I use that cloth?"

McGary hesitated, his voice filled with a gentle regret, "I'm sorry. It's a piece of my wife's dress— a keepsake, a memory of her."

Understanding the sentiment, Kane used his sleeve to wipe the glass; his hands still encased in mittens. An awkward silence settled between them.

"Ever been married?" McGary finally asked, leaving the question hanging heavy in the frigid air.

"Uncertain," Kane replied tersely. "She returned to her father's house when I embarked on this journey."

"A fate many sailors share," McGary remarked his tone a mix of resignation and reflection.

Lost in his thoughts, Kane resumed his meticulous record-keeping, with the surrounding silence echoing tales of unspoken emotions and quiet introspection.

Within the snug confines of the ship's mess, the crew huddled around the stove, seeking solace from the biting cold, while Kane and McGary conversed on the deck. Baker, a crew member with a soft spot for canines, tossed scraps to Old Grim, an endearing yet troublesome husky advanced in years. Petersen, choosing to lay in his bunk far from the stove, eyed the old dog.

"Why's Old Grim in here?" questioned Petersen, his gaze flitting between the husky and the crew. "Shouldn't he be with the pack on the ice?"

"He hates the cold," Baker replied, his eyes briefly meeting Hickey's. "He lurks by the door, sliding in at the first sign of an opening."

"That's his ploy," Petersen retorted. "The old, wart-covered, ring-boned thing feigns lameness until the sledge team is out of sight."

"Ever since the darkness cloaked us, he hides behind the gangway, only emerging to bid adieu when the departing teams are in the distance," Hickey added.

"He's a profound hypocrite, securing everyone's good graces and nobody's respect," Petersen sighed. "Younger dogs perish from unknown ailments, yet this old timer luxuriates in comfort. Throw him out."

With a hint of reluctance, Baker ushered Old Grim back on deck, but the husky soon found his way back, quietly resting just outside the door.

Weeks waned into an enveloping darkness, where Brooks and Petersen, swathed in layers, observed Kane clumsily handle a lamp on the deck.

"It seems even the lamps succumb to this frost," Kane mumbled.

"Our last reading marked it at minus sixty-seven," Brooks replied, his breath crystallizing in the freezing air.

"Two photographic plates, exposed at noon to the southern horizon, showed no trace of the sun."

"We shall try again in sixty days," decided Kane.

Moving along the deck, Kane unknowingly brushed the nose of a Newfoundland dog with his gloved hand. The minimal contact sparked excitement among the whole pack of dogs, who had quietly ascended the gangway and spread themselves on the deck. Kane and Brooks left them and went below. "The dogs have made their way to the deck," Petersen noted. "I'll herd them back to the ice."

"Let them stay," Kane intervened. "Their melancholy deepens with each passing day."

"They appear unaware of the flow of time," Petersen observed. "The absence of daylight dampens their spirits."

"To them, the sun has vanished for eternity," Kane mused. "We need to expose them to the lantern more frequently."

"This affliction, this seizure-like madness, is consuming them steadily," Brooks interjected.

"If we lose them all, our fate will be sealed," Petersen said gravely.

Returning to the deck, Brooks, Petersen, and Kane watched the dogs.

"Look!" Brooks exclaimed abruptly.

Flora, marked by her distinctive coat, barked at the unseen, pacing in curved lines like some strange dance.

"It's Flora, the wise one," Petersen pointed out.

Soon after, she crumpled to the ground, her jaw tightening, her body seized by convulsions.

"It has the look of rabies, yet Dr. Hayes insists it's something else," Brooks pondered. "It mimics lockjaw, yet it's distinctively different. It's utterly perplexing."

"What a heartbreaking loss," Kane murmured.

Leaving Petersen with Flora, Kane, and Brooks retreated inside, the gravity of the situation hanging heavy in the air. Petersen stayed, offering comfort to Flora in her last moments, preparing himself to do the inevitable.

In the ship's snug mess, a muted hum of activity pervaded the air the following day as individuals immersed themselves in various tasks. A dead rabbit dangled above the stove, slowly thawing, and buffalo robes hung, absorbing the warmth and airing by the stove's side.

Pierre, the French cook, shifted a few futile saucepans across the stovetop, his movements a blur of culinary adaptation. Meanwhile, others engaged in humble tasks, their minds and hands occupied to endure the protracted winter void. Brooks meticulously stitched canvas. Ohlsen carefully planned a board. Wilson and Whipple tenderly nursed two frail, mouse-colored Newfoundland dogs, feeding them minuscule spoonfuls of canned milk with maternal gentleness. Old Grim looked on in silence. Kane watched them all.

"Whipple. Your endeavors are in vain," Sontag declared, his voice laden with grim certitude. "Banish them to the deck and cease forming bonds with beings destined to perish in mere days."

"Let them stay," Kane responded gently. "If their days are numbered, let them experience joy." His words sparked a murmur of discontent from Sontag.

Sensing the building stress, Dr. Hayes diverted the conversation. "With the air at seventy-five below, and the sea-ice scarcely twenty-nine above, precise readings are impossible—the figures are of little worth."

Kane Inside Observatory

"Even with the observatory wrapped in sailcloth and a fire lit within, the temperature held at twenty below," Bonsall said. "And the flame skews the readings."

"Everything is frozen—the ether, naphtha, alcohol, wintergreen oil," Sontag replied, his tone caught between frustration and resignation. "Mark it 'too cold to measure.'"

"We must persist," Kane said. "If we fail to find Sir Franklin, these records will at least give weight to our work."

Weeks blended like colors on a canvas, their distinction lost to the freezing white abyss outside. The men, a motley crew of wanderers and explorers, had been brought together by fate and now found a sense of normality within the confines of their makeshift shelter. Once a mere corner with a few chairs and tables, the mess area had transformed into a sanctuary—a cocoon of safety amidst the ruthless arctic winds.

The shelter had been much altered. Exposed walls were now lined with stacked boxes, and heavy cloth hung for insulation. It was a rough fortress, made from whatever lay at hand, to hold what little warmth could be kept.

The men huddled around a battered stovetop, serving as their kitchen and heater. As the blue flame flickered, casting eerie shadows on their faces, stories of elation and sorrow were exchanged. Though spoken in hushed tones, these tales resonated with a gravity that only those faced with death could understand.

But amidst the camaraderie and shared meals, a heavy air of frustration persisted. The food supplies were depleting faster than expected, and the hunting expeditions were less fruitful than before. Hushed whispers became more frequent about dwindling rations and the looming unknown future.

Each night, as they settled into their sleeping bags, thoughts of home and warmth returned. The small shelter of wood, metal, and stoneware held unspoken hopes and quiet despair. Eyes once bright with the spirit of adventure now showed only uncertainty.

Yet, in the heart of the frozen wasteland, hope persisted. For as long as the flame burned, the men believed in a tomorrow. A tomorrow where the sun would shine brighter, the winds would be kinder, and their dreams of home would become a reality.

The unexpected departure of Old Grim was evidenced in their somber expressions. His breath turning to mist in the brisk air, Petersen bore the news with a heavy heart, and the group sank into profound silence, every man locked in his thoughts. Kane, suppressing the surge of anger and sorrow within, stepped into the moonlight. His emotions cascaded as he slammed the hatchway door open and vented his frustration by throwing an innocent pan.

He felt a pang of remorse as he stroked Toodlamick, his hand resting gently on her. The stillness matched his own quiet grief. "Sorry, Tood. Old Grim will be missed, won't he, girl?"

Kane looked out over the Arctic waste, his mind heavy with foreboding. "The next three months," he said, "will be a hard fight against this icebound wilderness." The words fell into silence, a sober warning of trials to come.

The brig had remained imprisoned in the eternal ice for three long, grueling months in the merciless grip of the Arctic frost. Cloaked in impenetrable darkness, she creaked hauntingly, her empty rigging swaying to the mournful melodies of the frigid wind. Each gust whispered tales of desolation.

X: Failed Search

Kane, his silhouette outlined against the unyielding darkness, paced restlessly beside the fire hole. His eyes were sharp, monitoring every action taken to ensure the hole remained unblocked and functional. In this icy expanse, each procedure was critical, a line between survival and disaster. Maintaining the fire hole, their safeguard against unforeseen blazes, was growing more challenging in the relentless cold.

Stevenson, his silhouette ghostly amidst the velvety shadows, approached Kane. Brooks and Petersen followed close on his heels, with the last of the loyal canines, Stumpy and Whitey, padding softly behind — mere phantoms in the enveloping darkness.

"Of the original forty-three, only six remain—and one is unfit for duty," Petersen said, his words hanging in the frost-heavy air.

Kane paused momentarily, his eyes reflecting the weight of the situation. "Then, we'll push forward with the remaining five," he finally said, his voice a blend of creeping dread and iron determination. "Mr. Brooks, come dawn, you will lead a team of seven men on foot. Utilize Ohlsen's newly improvised lighter sledge, ensuring it carries only the most vital provisions. We must extend our search, reaching as far north as the terrain allows."

"We'll also need to hunt during our search," Brooks interjected, his voice thick with grim acceptance.

"Agreed," Kane responded, his eyes steady, taking in the weary, shadowed faces around him, each marked by the trials of suffering and perseverance.

A week later, Kane stood firm on the deck, dressed for a journey into the unforgiving white expanse. His gaze fell upon the skeletal crew laboriously chipping away at the five-inch ice shield enveloping the deck. "It's been good insulation, but when the thaw comes, we'll be swamped. Our bunks below will be like swimming pools," Kane remarked to Hickey.

He then eyed the distinct color pattern of Hickey's gloves. "Are those Flora?" Kane inquired.

Hickey's grin bore both pride and melancholy. "They are. Captured her spirit exactly right. Are you setting out to scout for the search party?"

Kane's eyes scanned the frozen horizon. "We'll wait another week or two for them," he pronounced, the freezing air echoing the iciness in his words. "Today, however, I'm going hunting."

"Here's hoping you do better than Hans' recent attempts," Hickey quipped.

"Luck often trumps skill," Kane reflected. "Given the choice, I'd take fortune's favor any day."

With a rifle slung over his shoulder, Kane climbed the ridge that stretched upwards to a towering, rounded peak — a lone sentinel in the icy void, far removed from the brig. Reaching the summit, he caught his breath, not so much from the climb but from the draining effects of scant rations. Casting his gaze eastward, a fleeting flash of light caught his eye, a beacon of warmth in this frozen abyss. Heartened, Kane made his descent, a newfound hope kindling within him.

Bursting into the mess, Kane was confronted by the sight of his remaining crew. They appeared as mere shadows of the men they once were, their spirits sustained only by the faintest thread of hope, all yearning for the safe return of their comrades and a chance at salvation.

"I've witnessed it myself!" Kane's voice cut through the cold, silent air. "A ray of light broke through the relentless horizon! The sun is making its return, a beacon to end our isolation. We've triumphed over the endless night!"

Elation suddenly pierced the dense pall of despair that had long settled over the men. Cheers and jubilation echoed off the icy walls. Some of the men, those still possessing a shred of strength, displayed joy in spontaneous celebration. The ember of hope, smothered by endless days of pain and uncertainty, now blazed brightly, casting a beacon of light against the unfathomable darkness of the Arctic expanse.

A couple of days later, Kane sat at the mess table, skillfully stitching moccasins from skins dotted with white fur, his fingers deftly weaving through the material. Around him, the ambiance was one of domestic calm as fellow crew members immersed themselves in similar chores, finding a slice of normalcy within their icy refuge.

The sudden entrance of Sontag, Ohlsen, and Petersen shattered the fragile peace, their appearance akin to an unexpected storm. Their swollen hands and faces, marked by the ravages of hunger and cold, silently conveyed their harrowing ordeal. "What happened?" Kane's question pierced the tangible silence.

Initially, only their labored breaths spoke, each ragged inhalation echoing the toll of their ordeal. But then Ohlsen, his voice scarcely more than a tremulous whisper, found the strength to speak. "Left them... tent on the ice... defeated by the frost," he uttered between ragged breaths.

"Where?" Kane's voice was taut with urgency.

"Among the hummocks... forty hours northeast," Ohlsen managed, each word like a wisp of frost in the chilly air. "Snow's closing in... Morton's with them, but their hours are numbered."

"The dogs and sledge, are they with you?" Kane inquired further.

With a feeble nod, Ohlsen confirmed, "Yes."

Further questions were met with undeniable evidence of their exhaustion. The three men gave in to their fatigue, falling onto beds or directly to the floor, the weight of their ordeal still evident on their gaunt faces.

Compelled by urgency, Kane said, "My first thought is to leave at once. But in those shifting drifts, where do we begin?" His gaze turned to Ohlsen. "Is he fit to guide us?"

"I fear not," Hayes murmured, his eyes shadowed with concern.

"He must accompany us," Kane's voice was firm. "Only he knows the way if the tracks vanish. We'll wrap him in furs and secure him on the sledge to rest; his directions may be invaluable. We must leave without delay before the sledge tracks vanish."

Immediately, the crew sprang into action: some set about preparing a hasty meal, others gathered essential provisions for the rescue mission, while a few attended to the weakened arrivals. The atmosphere became thick with anticipation, with hope and trepidation swirling in the icy surroundings.

Rescue Party

The inky darkness enveloped the brig as a lone guardian amidst the frozen expanse. Within the hour, the active crew members, their forms highlighted by the dim light, prepared a sledge with utmost care.

They loaded a buffalo cover, a tent, a small alcohol stove, and pemmican. Ohlsen, still in a troubled sleep, was secured to the sledge and wrapped in furs. Kane called every able hand, leaving Whipple, Petersen, Sontag, and Dr. Hayes to tend the sick.

After an arduous day and a half, the relentless darkness obscured their vision, with treacherous ice hummocks impeding their path. McGary, hardly discernible amidst the shadows, urgently shook Ohlsen awake. Rousing to consciousness, Ohlsen was engulfed in a haze of confusion. Ohlsen's mind floundered as McGary and the crew sought guidance, providing no direction to the anxious group. The fierce winds and snow had erased any trace of the sledge tracks, stranding them in the merciless icy void.

"We can't be far—five, perhaps ten miles," Kane said, his voice cutting through the frozen air. "Rouse Ohlsen. Moving may keep the cold at bay. Melt ice for water, then spread out and search."

"The cold cuts like a knife—fifty below at least," McGary said. "The ice will not yield."

With Godfrey's assistance, Ohlsen, weakened, managed a few staggering steps, each one a struggle against the freezing grip. Bonsall handed out the precious pemmican while McGary tirelessly attempted to melt ice for water, and Hans worked on erecting their tent. Once the tent stood firm, Hans quickly ushered Ohlsen inside, providing a brief respite for his exhausted frame and overwhelmed mind against the ceaseless cold.

Settling in amidst the encompassing dark, the men spread out but stayed within Kane's vicinity, like celestial bodies orbiting a central star. Their continued efforts to melt ice were thwarted repeatedly. Bonsall, in desperation, tried eating snow, damaging his lips and tongue in the process. Bloodied and in pain, he was stopped by Kane's intervention. Finally, a hint of dawn began to touch the horizon, offering a glimmer of hope.

"McGary, Godfrey—get Ohlsen back to the sledge," Kane ordered. "Leave the tent. The rest of you, spread out and look for tracks."

Their nerves held them together like an invisible tether despite their intent to spread out. Their steps were cautious. The frigid silence interrupted only by the crunch of snow underfoot and their ragged breaths. McGary, Godfrey, and the looming presence of the sledge provided a constant, and even the dogs, sensing the unease, stayed close to Kane. Without warning, Bonsall started uncontrollably shivering, his breathing becoming distressingly shallow. Godfrey, struggling with balance, faltered repeatedly. And Kane, in a moment betraying his human vulnerability, lost his footing and was swallowed by a perilous snow drift, prompting a swift rescue effort by McGary and Hans.

Pushing against fatigue and the biting cold, the crew pressed on for another mile before Hans called out from ahead. "Mr. Kane—this may be a sledge track! See for yourself!"

Kane approached, every step heavy yet determined. "It's possibly just a rift, but right now, it's the most promising sign we've got," he declared, echoing hope and apprehension.

They chose the rift as their guide, and soon, distinct footprints emerged, winding their way through the snowy maze. The crew's anticipation surged, quickening their pace until, in the dim light, they spotted a humble American flag — a beacon amidst the white, marking a tent buried beneath the drifting snow's cold embrace.

Drawing from his last reserves of strength, Kane was the final one to approach. His crew, standing with reverence and trepidation, hadn't dared to enter the tent. They aligned themselves, forming a solemn corridor, motioning for Kane to take the lead into the unknown.

Kane entered the tent, the darkness immediately consuming him. He was met with a burst of weak yet heartfelt greetings from the men inside. Pierre's voice, though frail, held a note of hope. "We knew you'd come for us."

The magnitude of their situation struck Kane hard. Overwhelmed by emotions, he settled down among the afflicted men. With limited space, they huddled together, each man seeking warmth and comfort from the others.

Twelve hours later, the men began preparing for their return journey. They moved outside the tent, working on setting up the sledge. Ohlsen, still weak, managed to stand on shaky legs.

"Load the sick and what provisions remain onto the sledge," Kane said over the freezing wind. "Bring the tent—leave the rest."

The healthier men assisted their weaker comrades. Pierre tried to stand but failed, needing assistance to get onto the sledge. He and Wilson were swathed in furs, their frostbitten extremities a dark, concerning grey. Their condition was deteriorating, evident in their gaunt faces and weakened bodies. As the harsh environment continued its onslaught, the men began their challenging trek back to the Advance, facing biting wind and driving snow.

Their trek became a harrowing slog across tumultuous ice fields. The sledge, heavy and unyielding, required constant lifting and path-clearing through the ice. Despite the conditions, the dogs, especially Toodlamick and Whitey, showed remarkable resilience. Gale-force winds drove the snow into the men, the cold penetrating to their bones. Morton's eyes froze shut, his voice lost, leaving him with no more than a silent scream caught in his throat. As they battled onward,

Blake, overwhelmed by the harsh conditions, succumbed and collapsed into a snowdrift.

"We need the tent up immediately!" Kane's shout cut through the icy gusts. "McGary! Godfrey! Help!"

"Aye, Captain," McGary's voice was a lifeline amidst the storm's howl.

Bracing against the brutal winds, they wrestled the tent into position. Once inside, they huddled close, drawing warmth from one another, a makeshift refuge in a hostile landscape. After what felt like an eternity but was only a few hours, Kane stirred, nudging McGary.

"In here, a fire's too risky. I'll head to the tent we left halfway and melt ice and warm the pemmican," Kane whispered, glancing around their cramped quarters. "Join us in four hours."

He beckoned to Godfrey, his expression grave. Without another word, the pair ventured back into the freezing abyss.

Kane and Godfrey moved through the suffocating silence of the snowstorm, every step an exertion against nature's icy onslaught. As they pressed forward, Kane's instincts raised an alarm; a bear's tracks led toward the halfway tent. Upon arrival, they discovered the tent weighed down by snow, its form almost indistinguishable.

Raising it was taxing, their weary bodies protesting with every move. Once it was up, they burrowed into their sleeping bags, fighting the insidious cold that sought to rob them of warmth.

Upon waking, Kane's beard was a frozen tangle, frozen to the buffalo rug beneath him. "Godfrey," he rasped, "help me get loose. We need to melt some snow." Godfrey hovered over him for a heart-stopping moment, a knife glinting ominously. Kane met his gaze steadily, and after what felt like hours, Godfrey slashed not at him but at the rug, freeing him. They worked together, melting snow to provide vital, warm water.

By the time the rest of the group stumbled upon them, the storm had receded, leaving a deceptive calm. The warm water and pemmican rekindled a semblance of life in their starved bodies. Soon, they pressed on with renewed but fragile vigor, knowing home was still a formidable journey away.

Miles trudged on as hours waned until, finally, the silhouette of the brig materialized against the horizon. What initially seemed like a trick of weary eyes soon solidified, proving their sanctuary was within reach. A cacophony of raspy cheers erupted, each voice echoing the profound relief of a crew too long apart. Dr. Hayes, Petersen, and Whipple, alert to the distant noise, dashed forward, witnessing the poignant reunion of the frost-bitten survivors.

Every hand, however weary, partook in ushering the sick into the sheltering embrace of the ship. The harrowing ordeal etched into their souls, they had met the elemental fury and emerged, life coursing through their ice-chilled veins.

After ensuring the men were secured inside, Dr. Hayes employed friction and administered morphine to the incapacitated, while conversing with Kane, who, partially blinded by snow, strained to decipher his journal writings.

"The cerebral symptoms should recede soon," remarked Hayes. "The frostbite will persist."

"And Ohlsen?" asked Kane.

"He's battling scurvy," replied Hayes. "Likely to be blind for a duration. Pierre's lower leg is severely gangrenous; it's imperative to amputate it. Baker's recovery is uncertain."

"I'll help you with Pierre within the limits of my impaired vision," Kane offered. "Is there hope for Baker?"

"Not much more can be done," Hayes concluded.

"We've endured immense suffering," sighed Kane.

"What did you expect?" retorted Hayes. "It's miraculous that anyone survived this arduous journey."

Kane resumed his weary documentation as Hayes organized his surgical implements. "Hans has resilience; we should adapt his survival techniques," he mused.

Under ether's influence, Pierre was rendered unconscious for the amputation in the deep night. Kane supported his leg as Dr. Hayes performed the procedure, with some observing and others turning away.

Days later, the brig echoed with ominous gurgling from Baker, alerting all. Dr. Hayes and Kane rushed to his side, only to declare his passing. Silence enveloped them, shrouding the survivors in mourning.

First Winter Inside

As the late winter months progressed, they continued their searches as far north and west as their few remaining dogs would allow. Yet, no sign of Franklin had been found.

Clustered around the stove, the men pondered their dwindling resources. With spring showing no early signs of a thaw, the daunting prospect of enduring another harsh winter loomed. They longed for an early summer melt to allow them to retreat south. On top of these worries, the potential complications of encounters with the Esquimaux weighed heavily on their minds, even though Hans remained the only one of his kind they had come across.

"A rude awakening came that night as Dr. Hayes and McGary roused Kane with the grim news: Pierre had succumbed to infection. The loss shook Kane deeply. The shadow of death seemed ever closer.

The following day, the idea of a beacon in honor of their fallen comrades was proposed. Recognizing the importance of commemorating their hardships and losses, the crew agreed to the proposal. A ceremony was then held on Butler Island, attended by those physically able. Kane instructed Sven to inscribe a granite block with "ADVANCE A.D. 1853-54." This block was then set atop a stone pyramid marked by a painted Christian cross. They placed their expedition record inside the pyramid, sealed in a glass tube."

"Here we leave our legacy for future travelers," proclaimed Kane. "Now, our sole focus is our endurance through this next winter. Pursuing Franklin's traces takes second priority to our collective survival. Brace yourselves; this battle against the harsh winter demands our utmost courage and resolve."

The weight of Kane's proclamation hung in the air like an unshakable specter. Each passing day tightened their tether to the unforgiving Arctic. The relentless cold tested their resolve, and the realization that their survival now took precedence over their quest for Franklin's traces gnawed at their collective conscience. With Kane's words echoing in their minds, they knew their journey was far from over, and as they faced the uncertainties of the icy wilderness, the crew steeled themselves for the awaiting trials.

XI: Esquimaux Encounters

The next day, Dr. Hayes, Stevenson, and Morton were tidying Baker's area inside the brig. Kane remained in bed, ill and weighed down by a lingering sadness. The mood broke as Whipple rushed in from outside.

"Captain!" Whipple called urgently. "Come quickly!"

Kane got up as fast as his weakened body allowed. "What is it?" he inquired.

"They're here, sir," replied Whipple. "Hurry!"

Whipple quickly returned to the deck, with Kane first securing his pistol, and the others following closely behind.

On reaching the deck, they were met with a shocking sight: a group of disheveled and fierce-looking Esquimaux natives were aligned along the rocky shore, waving their arms and chanting in unison.

Meeting the Esquimaux

"Whipple, bring Petersen here," Kane instructed.

"From his bed?" Whipple questioned.

"Now!" Kane insisted. "Hans, stay with me."

Whipple dashed off, leaving the others facing the Esquimaux, who continued to hold their formation on the shore.

Once Petersen joined, Kane, Hans, and Petersen led a group of five men across the ice to confront the Esquimaux.

"Don't show weakness," Kane warned.

Kane revealed his open hands to the natives' leader, who he presumed by the man's stature and central position. The imposing Esquimaux, Metek, advanced to meet Kane. He was tall and powerfully built, with a weathered face and sharp black eyes. He was dressed in a mixed fur hooded jumper and white bearskin trousers, bear claws protruding from his boots. The other Esquimaux surrounded Metek, Kane, and his team.

"Invite him on board, but make sure the others stay here," Kane said to Petersen.

Petersen conversed with Metek in their language, receiving a nod in reply.

"He's called Metek," Petersen informed.

Under an uneasy truce, Kane led Metek into the men's living quarters. Metek's kin followed closely, their unbridled curiosity sending them exploring every nook and cranny despite Kane's explicit instructions. With a silent plea from Kane, Dr. Hayes gathered the infirm, further heightening the ambient apprehension.

The Esquimaux moved with unrestrained curiosity, their spirited conversations and ceaseless movements filling every corner of the ship. Kane's men had their hands full trying to manage these unexpected guests, but they did so without any major confrontations.

The Esquimaux were quick to transfer items to their sledges, frequently returning to barter or trade. Amidst this whirlwind, McGary worked diligently, reclaiming essential things swept up in the flurry of exchanges. McGary noticed that the Esquimaux sledges were much superior to their Greenland ones.

In time, both crew and visitors gathered around the stove, a fleeting camaraderie taking shape. The Esquimaux hungrily devoured their raw walrus meat, eyes widening as Whipple roasted some over the coal fire. Their enthusiasm for the meal was unmatched, overshadowing even the appetites of Kane's men. But just as suddenly as their feast began, a heavy drowsiness claimed the visitors. They slumped in place, resting deeply, with remnants of their meal at their sides. The scene left Kane and his crew in quiet amazement.

Kane, Petersen, and Metek sat on crates the following morning. Kane revealed a small box to establish rapport, presenting needles and beads to Metek. Having become more aligned with the crew's ways, Hans kept a watchful distance from these visitors, echoes of his lineage.

Tension hung in the air as both sides cautiously tried to understand the other. Every look and gesture carried weight as they silently assessed each other's intentions. The Esquimaux, with a blend of curiosity and caution, took in the unfamiliar surroundings while Kane's men, equally intrigued, scrutinized their unexpected guests. At this moment, two worlds were colliding, filled with silent hopes and uncertainties.

"See if they're willing to exchange their walrus meat and dogs for more items like these," Kane suggested to Petersen, his voice maintaining a firm but inquisitive tone.

Translating for Kane, Petersen communicated the proposal to Metek. After considering the beads and needles, Metek's eyes lingered on some empty casks near the brig.

"He desires those empty casks as well," relayed Petersen.

"And the dogs, for our explorations?" pressed Kane.

"Once their hunt concludes, their dogs and sledges will be at your disposal," Petersen relayed, post translation.

"A favorable outcome," mused Kane, "if their words hold sincerity."

The assembly of Esquimaux prepared to depart.

Kane and Petersen silently contemplated as the Esquimaux, alongside their dogs, ventured across the icy expanse. "I wonder what malice they might harbor," Kane murmured.

As the silhouettes of the Esquimaux blended with the southern horizon, Morton approached Kane from the opposing direction. "Several artifacts have vanished from the observatory: axes, saws, knives…" Morton reported.

"There's your answer," uttered Petersen, his words tinged with subtle concern.

A few days, hence, five Esquimaux emerged adjacent to the brig. Kane, Brooks, and Petersen engaged with them from the deck.

"Mr. Petersen, forbid their entry aboard," commanded Kane. "Insist upon the return of the appropriated items."

Petersen relayed the demand, but while the Esquimaux understood his words, they missed their deeper meaning, resulting in a bewildered retreat. Subsequent sporadic disappearances of assorted items only heightened Kane's concerns about survival. The steady loss of essential tools and resources threatened to be the difference between life and death in the coming winter. Yet, Kane was reluctant to spark a conflict.

Amid the growing unease within the crew and the silent battles of survival that Kane and his men waged, the interaction with the Esquimaux had evolved into a precarious balance of danger, misunderstanding and desperation. Each encounter held the potential for mutual assistance or mutual destruction, as the language barrier and the stark contrast in their needs often resulted in confusion and mistrust. As the crew strove to guard their dwindling stores, another tense meeting on Butler Island cast a shadow over the fragile rapport that had begun to take shape..

XII. Kane's Struggle

In the sunlit observatory on Butler Island, McGary and Morton, huddled over their instruments, heard the encroaching footsteps of the Esquimaux. They swiftly took cover in the shadows of their makeshift hut, spotting three Esquimaux attempting to steal a barrel of coal. As they weighed their options, an Eider duck flew overhead. Seizing the moment, Morton fired his gun, felling the bird. The gunshot's echo filled the air, and the Esquimaux, paralyzed by the display of firepower, fled in terror, not daring to look back. "Looks like guns are unknown to them," deduced Morton.

The sharp crack of the gunshot still echoed in their ears. McGary glanced at Morton, a hint of admiration in his eyes. "That shot served two goals," McGary mused, lifting the fallen Eider. "meal for us and a message to our visitors."

Morton smirked. "It sure prompted a swift retreat. And, fortunately, an Eider is now our gain."

The shadows lengthened on the ship's deck, wrapping everything in a hazy, dim light. Brooks and Petersen stood guard, their silhouettes sharp against the encroaching darkness. Every rustle, every whisper of the wind heightened their senses, the diminished daylight reminding them of the need for extreme vigilance.

Suddenly, the sound of sledge runners slicing through the snow caught their attention. Approaching was a youthful and sprightly Esquimaux, Myouk, his demeanor a stark contrast to the earlier interlopers. His team of dogs, well-fed and energetic, were hitched to a heavily laden sledge.

Brooks alerted the crew, his voice carrying a note of cautious curiosity.

"Company approaching!" Crew members emerged from the ship's belly and converged around the newcomer. Myouk flashed a cheeky grin, his eyes sparkling with mischief and a touch of bravado. The crew's mood was like a thin, rubber-like line stretched between curiosity and wariness.

The frigid wind carried the distant howls of sledge dogs, setting the atmosphere taut with unease. "Interrogate the boy about our missing India-rubber boat," Brooks sternly directed Petersen. Though patient and deliberate, Petersen's questions flounder upon Myouk's limited comprehension. The more they tried to bridge the communication gap, the more frustration mounted.

"We can't let this go," Brooks said, his voice icy with determination. "Secure him in the hold. Either he finds his voice and conscience, or perhaps his kin will come forward to reclaim him."

Myouk's eyes widened in realization. As the crew approached, a sense of desperation enveloped him. His struggles were vigorous but futile, and he was quickly led into the ship's bowels.

Below deck, the metallic clinks of chains punctuated the stillness. Myouk, though restrained, projected a spirit unyielding. His mournful cries, echoing through the timber and steel, evoked a raw pain. Each sob bore a tale, and amidst this heart-rending backdrop, his story surfaced. Whispered words of an abode in 'Etah' and of kin waiting for his return painted a poignant picture, stirring a dilemma within Kane's heart.

The freezing morning dawned with new uncertainties. The vacancy where Myouk had been confined was a tangible reminder of Kane's decision, which left some crew members disconcerted. As they gathered for breakfast, their whispered conversations revealed a shared unease.

After breaking a contemplative silence, Petersen asked, "Has everyone heard about Myouk's departure?"

Kane, his voice edged with concern, queried, "What did he manage to take with him?"

"Only what was originally his," McGary replied, his eyes darting distrustfully toward the deck.

Kane took a deep breath, exhaling the mist of strain. "We walk a tightrope of challenges and choices. We must stay resolute and not be derailed by distractions. Our eyes and minds must remain sharp."

The men grappled with personal and collective challenges as days wore on. During one icy morning, a visibly weary Kane, bearing the signs of his recent hunting endeavors, engaged Brooks in conversation.

"Our immediate needs, our drive to sustain ourselves, seem to eclipse our broader mission," commented Brooks, his words punctuated by the frost in his beard.

Kane, weariness evident in his gaze, agreed. "Our immediate necessities shape our actions."

Looking at the expansive white horizon, Godfrey mused aloud, "Could the Esquimaux have helped Sir Franklin's crew survive?"

Still lost in the vastness before him, Kane replied, "Would their inherent nature permit such a gesture of goodwill?"

"And Sir Franklin," Godfrey continued, "Could he have amassed enough supplies to withstand back-to-back winters and eventually find his way home?"

But it was McGary, his tone as biting as the chill around them, who posed the most unsettling question, "The real conundrum is: can we?"

A shiver, more from the weight of that question than the cold, ran through Kane. He recognized the need to bolster his crew's spirits. They stared at the prospect of another relentless winter if the ship remained trapped. Yet, Kane knew that with the advent of spring, despite the odds, they would resume their search for Franklin, propelled by undying hope and unwavering determination.

The fleeting embrace of the Arctic summer came and went in a mere six weeks. Search parties veered north and west, reserving the southern expanse for their eventual departure, but the elusive traces of Franklin and his crew remained hidden from their desperate search.

XIII. Godfrey Departs

The days began to dim, losing their length again to the inevitable embrace of Arctic winter. One evening, Kane called the men to a briefing around the stove.

Bonsall, Brooks, Kane, Hayes and Morton

"Come sunrise, we'll commence the gathering of moss for fuel. We'll submerge willow stems and sorrel in the snow beside the ship to..." Kane's voice was firm, resonant, but suddenly interrupted by Godfrey.

"We intend to journey south on foot," he declared, his tone resolute. "We've debated this, and consensus resides with me."

Petersen and Riley rose, signifying their agreement, though Riley sat back down.

"My numerous encounters with the Arctic have convinced me of this course," asserted Petersen.

"This reeks of mutiny!" Hickey's voice, a clash of fear and defiance, cracked through the air.

"Legally, it's not," retorted Brooks calmly. "Nautical law dictates that a beset ship relinquishes the master's authority, allowing the crew to determine their counsel."

Kane rose, his demeanor composed yet stern.

"This isn't mutiny, but it's imprudent," he affirmed. "My duty as captain binds me to this brig as long as a shred of recovery hope lingers. However, your obligation doesn't mirror mine. Thus, I can release you officially from your duties on the ship. I'll deliver my final response come morning."

As the Arctic winds whispered through the silent night, Dr. Hayes approached Kane, immersed in contemplation, leaning against the railing overlooking the boundless ice.

"Our preparedness for another winter onboard is lamentably inadequate," Kane murmured.

"We are a band of scurvy-afflicted, weary men," conceded Hayes.

"Our provisions are critically diminished in quantity and quality," added Kane.

"True, but the vitality of men's spirits is crucial for their survival come next spring," argued Hayes. "A spirit laced with reluctance, despair, and dejection will likely be more fatal than any plague."

"Pushing men to their limits, against their judgment, can be equally damaging to their spirit and resolve," Kane retorted, his voice a mixture of frustration and understanding.

Their gazes met, a silent exchange of resolve and concern, as their situation weighed down on them both.

With dawn, the crew congregated on the deck, the ailing among them, all eyes expectant, awaiting Kane's judgment.

"Setting our course south at this juncture, with winter on our heels, is fraught with peril," Kane began, his tone somber.

Godfrey interrupted, voice laden with anguish, "Your cautious approach has drained us! Remaining here is a death sentence!" A murmur of concurrence swept through the assembly.

Kane raised his hand for silence, his voice carrying an earnest plea, "I urge you all to reconsider. We mustn't let fear cloud our judgment."

But Godfrey was unyielding. "The South beckons with a chance at life. Here, we are chained to indecision and impending doom." His voice trembled with anger, despair, and faint hope.

Kane took a deep breath, exhaling slowly, "The choice is yours. My door remains open for those who wish to discuss the dangers that lie in fleeing."

Godfrey's scoff cut through the charged atmosphere, the heavy silence on deck broken only by the sound of anxious breaths and shifting feet. Every man seemed to be internally wrestling, balancing his fears with the impending decision.

"Those willing to embark on this perilous journey south will be provided with a fair allocation of our remaining provisions and our collective best wishes," Kane proclaimed. This assurance brought a fleeting sigh of relief among the crew, the previously taut strings of tension easing momentarily.

Kane, however, wasn't finished. "I stipulate two conditions: First, you will select a single person from your ranks to lead your group. Second, in return, you will formally forgo any rights or claims upon those of us who elect to remain with the ship." His voice held a tone of somber gravity, underscoring the irreversible nature of the split.

Godfrey's sneer was audible. "To your last breath, you'll clutch to order and regulation, even if it's your downfall on this desolate ice."

Brooks, ever the peacemaker, intervened, "It's about maintaining a semblance of order, even in chaos."

Kane's gaze swept over the men. "We'll now conduct a roll call. You'll declare your choice and then sign this document as a testament to your decision."

A ripple of anxious titters passed through the crew. As names were called, men shuffled to align with Kane or Godfrey. In a move that spoke louder than words, Dr. Hayes stepped forward unprompted, signing the document with deliberate intent.

With a heavy heart, Kane surveyed the group—Sontag, Bonsall, Hayes, Whipple, Riley, Petersen, Stevenson, and Blake—aligning with Godfrey.

"Now, let's expedite preparations to maximize the remaining daylight," urged Kane.

The departing assembly spent the better part of a day accumulating the required provisions and sustenance.

Dr. Hayes pulled Kane aside. "I'm going with them, not as a matter of loyalty," he said quietly. "They'll need my care out there, and you have the training to manage the medical needs here."

On the frost-laden ice the following morning, Kane extended a letter to the newly designated leader, Godfrey.

"This letter details the specifics of your departure," Kane articulated somberly in the icy silence. "It carries our promise of a fraternal welcome should fate force your return. Lead them well, Mr. Godfrey."

Godfrey, his eyes betraying myriad emotions, silently accepted the letter, clutching it firmly, and turned away.

"Sir, you have always been a beacon of strength. We leave with hopes of your well-being in the daunting months ahead and the prayer that we all find what we seek," expressed Dr. Hayes, his tone laced with respect and a sorrowful farewell.

The contingent embarked on their journey, their figures gradually blurring into the endless white horizon, leaving those who stayed to reflect on the shrinking fraternity, the weakened and ailing, the depleting resources, the looming shadow of another frigid night, and the intensified solitude. Kane's thoughts lingered on the uncertainties and fears that were clouding the minds of those who had ventured into the unknown.

XIV. Harrowing Winter

Dawn had barely broken when the men, cornered by their circumstances, found renewed resolve amidst despair. The threat of disaster can revive even the most lethargic spirit.

"Regardless of the challenges," asserted Kane, his voice steely against the cold, "routine is our weapon against despair and our fortress against dwindling morale. Our existence will remain rhythmic and disciplined, with meals, fires, and watches marking our days."

"Our routine remains?" asked Brooks, searching Kane's eyes.

"Mostly," replied Kane. "We need to adapt for survival. Beginning today, everyone will contribute to collecting moss and turf."

"Why moss and turf?" Brooks' confusion was clear.

"Start immediately, and the reason will become clear," Kane advised.

The icy shore echoed their labor as they tirelessly worked the frozen ground. Under the deck, they carved a small sanctuary, insulating it with the blocks of moss and turf they had extracted.

"These blocks ensure our survival," said Brooks.

"Once it's done, we'll insulate the brig with snow," Kane explained.

Gathering Moss

With their directions set, the men set to work. Their labor was continuous, the frozen earth yielding to their effort. The transformation of their living space into an icy haven was a testament to their adaptability and an exercise in survival.

The next day, as Brooks watched, Kane and Hans prepared to embark into the icy expanses. Kane, now resembling an Esquimaux in attire crafted by Hans, voiced his concerns: "Game is dwindling. Our journey might be long and returns uncertain. Stay vigilant. Any loss could be devastating."

With those words, Kane and Hans delved deeper into the icy wilderness. For miles and miles, their journey was marked by silence until Hans exclaimed, "Seals!" Spotting seals was a welcome sight, but the joy was short-lived. As they neared the animals, the sledges navigated onto treacherous ice. The surrounding landscape was filled with unreliable ice patches. They could not stop. Every move they made was dangerous, and the risk of the ice breaking beneath them was undeniably high.

A distant lump of solid ice appeared as a beacon of hope during their perilous journey, as though nature extended a lifeline, a sliver of safety amidst their treacherous path. But the refuge floated over a mile away. There was no turning back; moving forward was the only option.

"Keep going."

Sensing the urgency, the dogs scrambled forward, their quickened breaths muffling their anxious whimpers.

"Don't let them stop!" Kane shouted, his voice competing against the cracking ice.

Their salvation lay in reaching the distant lump of solid ice. A pause could prove fatal. Curiously, seals popped out of the water, watching the desperate race.

But the sprint had its limits. The unstable ice beneath them heightened the dogs' anxiety. Just shy of safety, panic froze the dogs in their tracks. Disaster struck: the sledge's left runner broke through the ice, dragging Toodla and part of their supplies into the freezing abyss. Acting swiftly, Kane tried freeing Toodla but was pulled into the water.

"Got! Got!" Hans cried, invoking the Almighty.

"Lie down! Spread out! Use your knife!" Kane managed to yell amidst the chaos.

Kane, partially submerged alongside Toodla, worked frantically to free her. As Toodla was liberated, the numbing cold slowed Kane's actions, causing his knife to slip from his grasp.

Hans, uttering prayers in a mix of languages, watched in sheer horror. Toodla, still tethered to the sledge but now on the ice, managed to position one of its runners onto firmer ground. Seizing this lifeline, Kane used the runner to haul himself up, contending with both the pull of the frigid water and the fragile, breaking ice. With

Toodla's assistance, Kane pulled himself to safety. Once on solid ice, he promptly untied Toodla. Together, they trudged towards more stable ground, their spirits burdened yet grateful.

Turf Walls Within Hull

Back at the brig, inside their turf shelter, Kane sat near the stove, deep in reflection. McGary, the only other soul awake, sat by his side.

"If I had worn my usual attire, the weight would've pulled me under," Kane mused.

"An Esquimaux survival tactic?" McGary responded.

Kane, lost in thought, took down Sir Franklin's picture from the wall.

XV. Esquimaux Return

In an atmosphere pregnant with the strain of survival, the appearance of three Esquimaux near the brig ignited a fresh flame of tension. Brooks and McGary, standing guard, exchanged glances as the newcomers approached, their shadows looming on the icy landscape. McGary, with measured steps, attempted communication.

"They seek shelter for the night," McGary relayed upon his return.

"Let them camp on the ice," Kane directed. "Provide them a copper lamp, a basin, and fuel slush, but restrict their access to the deck during the night."

Brooks' eyes flickered with concern, "Fuel is scarce."

"It's a necessity," Kane insisted. "We may require their assistance soon."

The air grew heavier, whispers of mistrust circulating among the men. Riley returned unexpectedly, his presence initiating a tense pause before Brooks handed him a load of turf to carry. The silence spoke volumes as the men continued their relentless labor. Riley blended back in like he had never gone.

By the next dawn, the men discovered the unsettling absence of their possessions and their strongest dog, Nanook. Kane's voice broke the men's murmurings: "This hostility must cease immediately!"

But the glaring question was how to cease it. Kane's eyes were steadfast. "Arm Morton and Wilson. Have them track them and recover everything."

Under the cover of night, the two seamen stealthily approached a small Esquimaux village. The presence of Nanook confirmed their suspicions. A tense whisper from Morton, "Prepare for confrontation," preceded the drawing of pistols.

Inside, Myouk, Sievu, and Aningna remained oblivious to the impending confrontation. Morton and Wilson expertly captured and corralled the unsuspecting Esquimaux onto two sledges along with their ill-gotten possessions.

The dawn revealed the three captives in Advance's improvised holding cell, with Brooks standing over them with his gun. His voice reverberated through the ship as he berated Myouk. The air was thick with anxiety, Myouk's eyes radiating fear under the threat of Brooks' gun.

"No 'fire death!'" His plea echoed, drawing Kane and McGary to the scene.

"Enough!" Kane's voice thundered, shattering the tension that had gripped the room. His penetrating gaze bore into Myouk as if attempting to uncover the motivations behind the thefts.

"Does he even comprehend our need for those possessions?" McGary's translations painted a picture of Myouk's mindset, which seemed to lack the idea of ownership, leaning more towards borrowing or community property rather than theft.

Deep in contemplation, Kane finally spoke, "Their actions aren't fueled by malice but by a fundamental misunderstanding of possession. To them, trading is simply an exchange of use, not a claim of ownership."

As these words settled in, a faint understanding began to pierce through the veil of uncertainty and hostility that had enveloped the room. It was a fragile moment, a tentative step towards bridging the chasm that separated the two worlds struggling to survive.

"So, they have no concept of right or wrong?" Brooks pondered aloud.

Kane's expression remained resolute. "Regardless, we must put an end to their 'borrowings.'"

As they considered the path ahead in this intricate web of survival and cultural differences, the air hung heavy with unspoken questions and unresolved conflict.

"How do we manage that?" inquired McGary.

"Communicate on their terms," Kane decided. "Instead of waiting for spring, let's send a team to 'Etah' immediately with a proposition for Metek, their leader, emphasizing our superior barter options."

"Yet, that might not resolve the core issue," McGary said. "They may continue to 'borrow.'"

"Then we need to explain our norms," replied Kane. "Learning is a two-way street. Release Myouk to convey our message to their leader for a meeting while keeping the others as collateral."

Ten days later, Metek arrived with a sizable entourage of Esquimaux, bearing a sledge-load of knives, tin cups, bits of wood, scraps of iron, and various other items that had been "borrowed." Kane's crew retrieved and stowed their belongings.

To address the concern of their overwhelming numbers, Kane deliberately displayed firearms, leaving no doubt in the minds of the Esquimaux about the superior force they were facing. Metek took the initiative in the conversation, first speaking with Sievu. After securing his crew's safety and asserting their superiority, Kane initiated a peace talk with Metek, stressing the significance of respect for each other's needs.

"Make sure our position is absolutely clear," Kane instructed McGary.

Kane's voice thundered, cutting through the hostile atmosphere. He demanded answers; his eyes locked onto Myouk, who stood before him, a picture of trepidation.

McGary, the interpreter, strained to bridge the linguistic and cultural gap. "Does he even grasp our need for those possessions?" he asked.

The translation painted a picture of Myouk's mindset, which lacked ownership, leaning more toward borrowing rather than outright theft. But understanding didn't erase mistrust.

Kane, his gaze following the departing figures, felt the weight of uncertainty, contemplating the evolving dynamics and potential dangers that lingered on the horizon with the Esquimaux. The precarious balance achieved seemed like a beacon of transient hope in the tenuous relationship intertwined with contrasting perceptions and mutual survival.

XVI. Calamity Strikes

Amid the relentless chill of the second winter, a perpetual haze of dim light and shadow shrouded their days. The men worked tirelessly on the icy terrain, their efforts intertwined with the fate of their trusty brig. An improvised quadrangular blockhouse arose from this relentless toil, fashioned from barrels that once held their dwindling supplies—beef, pork, flour, beans, and dried apples. Proudly soaring in one corner was their flagstaff, bearing the American flag adorned with 27 stars and 13 red and white stripes—a stoic emblem of unwavering loyalty to their purpose and determination.

Flanked by boats and stacks of cut wood, the blockhouse extended like a crude avenue at a right angle from the side of the brig's hull. Filled with hope and longing, McGary erected a signpost for the area he christened "New London," with an arrow beneath pointing toward Washington, some 5,500 miles away. On either side of the entryway, Toodla and Young Whitey, the lead dogs, stood sentinel-like, guarding the passage as if entrusted with a sacred duty.

Beyond this makeshift boundary, a hut constructed from barrel frames and snow served as a welcoming area for potential Esquimaux visitors. A rope barrier firmly demarcated the limits of their territory, a stark line drawn between their world and the realm of the "civilized."

"Mr. Goodfellow, keep a sharp watch," Kane cautioned. "Our provisions may attract bears."

Goodfellow responded with concern, "We've relocated our food stores to evade the small brown rats, but now we must guard against the large white ones. At this rate, our provisions won't last much longer."

Hickey added with frustration in his voice, "The rats are devouring everything—furs, woolens, shoes, even our precious specimens. Beyond the cold and scurvy, we're plagued by three Arctic curses: rats, rats, and more rats."

Kane responded firmly and decisively, "Once those rodents are plump enough, we'll eat them."

"Inside, we're maintaining a temperature of forty-five degrees, even with only four hours of fire each night," Brooks reported, his words carrying a hint of relief. "So far, the moss is holding up."

Kane, his expression focused, concluded his calculations, "Based on Ohlsen's report, we can extract another eight tons of fuel from the hull without compromising her seaworthiness."

McGary, his voice a delicate balance between hope and caution, added, "With some reinforcement to the main hatch with canvas and strategic modifications to the entryway, we should endure the upcoming extremes."

Each day unfolded as the crew navigated the treacherous path between survival and surrender. Their unwavering resolve waged an unspoken war against the biting cold and the unseen threats lurking in the shadows. Their collective heartbeat echoed with determination to confront and conquer the Arctic's curses.

"Except for scurvy," Brooks sighed. "It will continue to haunt us, even after the return of light and vegetation in late April."

"With Morton, Hans, and Wilson down and the endless night beginning again, you two must hold on," Kane reminded them, his voice tinged with somber acknowledgment.

McGary nodded, his gaze fixed on the desolate landscape. "We're about to face the hardest six months of our lives, undoubtedly."

Late into the night, within their makeshift igloo, the stove emitted a glow as vivid as a ripe cherry, casting a faint red hue across their faces. The air in the confined space was dense with tension, weighing heavily on Brooks, Wilson, Morton, and Goodfellow. Their bodies, besieged by scurvy, languished in their bunks. The walls and ceiling, stained black by soot and moisture, wept droplets onto the bedclothes and the table where Kane sat, immersed in his writing.

"I need to check the traps," Kane declared, his voice cutting through the stillness like a knife.

Hans, who had recently recovered, replied with a voice filled with concern, "I can do it, Captain. You don't need to go out in this bitter cold."

Kane contemplated momentarily and then decided, "I'll have Hans accompany me."

Hours later, as they braved the biting cold and enveloping darkness, Hans and Kane embarked on their expedition to inspect the desolate traps scattered about two miles from the brig along the icy terrain. Their footfalls on the crisp snow pierced the silence, their sound echoing through the vast desolation. A deafening roar, monstrous and bone-chilling, suddenly shattered the stillness, leaving them frozen in their tracks.

"Hans, do you share my thoughts?" Kane asked, his breath visible in the frigid air.

Another roar, louder and closer, rumbled through the darkness. The two men exchanged fearful glances in the pitch-black night.

"Yes! Yes!" Hans's whisper was barely audible. "It's Nanook."

Walking along the edge of the five-foot-high ledge of the icefoot, they leaped up to grab the lip, pulled themselves onto it, and lay down, facing outward to scan the icy expanse. Anxiety radiated through their frozen bodies as their eyes meticulously scanned the darkness. At first, all they saw was an eerie stillness. The anticipation grew, and finally, they discerned a subtle movement—was it a shifting mound of ice?

Kane examined his small-caliber pistol, shaking his head in silent acknowledgment of its inadequacy.

"Why did we forget to bring a rifle?" Kane murmured to himself. "One of us must act as bait."

Hans, puzzled, asked in a hushed tone, "What is 'bait'?"

Kane explained quickly, "I'll divert the bear's attention; you run back to the brig and fetch a rifle. The men depend on their hunter more than me."

"No," Hans interjected, his face determined. "I will be the decoy. You run."

"Hans, return to the brig. Secure a rifle. I'll divert Nanook," Kane urged.

"No," Hans smiled resolutely. "The men need their captain."

A third roar, resounding and potent, confirmed the bear's menacing proximity. An unspoken understanding passed between them, and together, they sprinted through the uneven terrain, their movements erratic, hearts pounding. The looming shadow of the pursuing bear served as a relentless reminder of the imminent threat it posed. Kane, discarding his mittens one by one to gain precious seconds, led the way as the bear appeared to be herding them, toying with them as they neared the brig.

On the brig's deck, McGary caught sight of the sprinting figures and quickly grabbed a rifle. But when he raised it to fire, the bear had vanished. The men stopped at the gangplank and looked back in bewilderment. Ohlsen burst out of the stairwell, his face etched with concern. Smoke billowed out from the doorway behind him.

"Captain! Captain!" Ohlsen shouted. "Fire! Come quickly!"

Kane and McGary bounded up the gangplank and descended into the hatchway, their hearts racing as they faced yet another unexpected challenge in the relentless struggle for survival.

Below deck, Kane beheld a dire scene. The bulkhead blazed with fierce intensity, dry timbers crackling like malevolent laughter as they succumbed to the flames, and the very skin of the brig seemed poised to ignite. The moss-wall, one side of their sleeping quarters, and the store of rifles and gunpowder teetered perilously close to the ravenous fire.

"Form a line to the fire-hole, swiftly!" Kane barked, his voice a desperate plea. "Pass water quickly. Hans, Ohlsen, defend the moss wall!"

With unwavering determination etched across their faces, Kane, Hans, and Ohlsen plunged headlong into the fiery sailcloth that formed the walls of their storeroom. They fought ferociously, using skins to beat back the relentless flames. In a bold move, Kane thrust himself through the fiery barrier to kick a barrel of gunpowder away from the raging inferno, falling amidst the blaze. Undaunted by the searing heat, Hans rushed to his aid, and together, they battled the relentless blaze with soaked furs until McGary arrived with the first bucketful of water. The clash between water and flames birthed clouds of steam and smoke, momentarily overwhelming Kane.

He staggered toward the hatchway, fighting dwindling consciousness, falling against Ohlsen's legs. With strength born of desperation, Ohlsen hoisted him up to the deck—Kane's beard singed, eyebrows mostly vanished, and his forehead and palms burned crimson. The relentless efforts of the men finally subdued the fire. The ship was saved.

"What started it," Kane asked.

"There's been theft among our supplies," McGary revealed, his voice heavy with concern. "I discovered melted wax—evidently from a candle."

"If it was Godfrey, I will tear him to shreds," Ohlsen warned vehemently.

In the enveloping darkness of the evening, Hans stood next to Kane, lying on the deck, still recovering from smoke inhalation.

"Nanook save us," Hans mused.

"What do you mean?" Kane inquired weakly.

"He drove us back to see the fire," Hans clarified.

Kane, his mind a whirl of thoughts, cocked his head, conceding partially to Hans's insight.

That night, by the flickering lamplight, Kane lay weakened near the stove, meticulously charting their progress. Wilson, his legs ravaged by scurvy, tended to the dishes. Morton and Brooks, despite their deteriorating health, stitched new fur clothing. Goodfellow lost in delirium, lay in his bunk, his teeth grinding and words spilling uncontrollably.

"We must address McGary and Riley's scurvy immediately," Kane whispered to Brooks.

"My concerns are more about Morton," replied Brooks gravely. "Conducting surgery on his perforated Achilles tendon in these conditions could induce lockjaw."

"We cannot afford to lose anyone," Kane stressed. "We require every man in optimal health if we harbor any hopes of departure."

After days that drifted on, one evening, within the softly lit daytime igloo, Morton's face bore the marks of suffering as he propped himself up on one elbow, his eyes following the bustling activity around him.

"We've managed to chop the wood, Gotdamn! Twenty-four hundred pounds," Ohlsen announced proudly as he came in. "It should hold us until January."

"Aye, with the harshest two months yet to descend upon us," retorted Morton, his voice tinged with grim amusement.

"We still have the outer oak as well," Kane reminded.

"Yeah," agreed Ohlsen, "Slash it to the waterline, and we'll gather tons more. And, the brig will maintain her seaworthiness."

"Indeed, provided we dodge the waves," interjected Morton dryly.

"With providence on our side, we shall endure the winter and preserve the brig," affirmed Kane, his eyes carrying a spark of hopeful resolve.

Weeks rolled by, and all men found solace within the reconstructed igloo except those on vigilant deck watch. The renovation of the internal igloo included a narrower entrance, a modification designed to trap more warmth within its icy walls. Kane sat at the crudely fashioned table, swathed in furs, his quill scribbling in the ship's log. He stopped writing momentarily to pare part of a potato and share it with McGary. Soot marred every face, a testament to the smoky emissions from their stove.

"Only a dozen remain," Kane murmured, referring to the potatoes, his voice filled with reverence and melancholy. "Frozen relics of the dear land they hail from, three years and counting."

"Their shield against scurvy is more precious than gold in these realms," declared McGary.

"The ways of the Esquimaux perplex me," mused Kane. "Their possessions are meager, their innovations derived from all they stumble upon, yet they harbor no foresight for their ensuing needs."

A voice pierced the icy silence from the deck above, "Captain! Esquimaux sledges approach."

Kane's thoughts shifted to a tangled web of curiosity and cautious optimism. The arrival of the Esquimaux sledges might present a new chapter in their frozen story. The grime-covered faces of the crew silently considered the mysteries and potential revelations the visitors might carry with them.

XVII. Prodigal Return

Emerging from the shelter of the brig, Kane, Ohlsen, and McGary, their bodies weakened but spirits undaunted, limped onto the deck to join Riley. Their eyes remained fixed on five sledges approaching rapidly. The drivers of these sledges were unknown entities, except for Myouk and two familiar passengers, Petersen and Bonsall, remnants from the party that had departed earlier. The Esquimaux assisted the men inside with an air of silent understanding. Myouk, with a mysterious glint in his eyes, playfully tweaked Kane's cheek in passing, leaving Kane bemused and pondering the gesture's significance.

Within the confines of the brig, Petersen and Bonsall, a mix of embarrassment and fatigue evident in their demeanor, conversed in frail voices.

"Our journey painfully validated all the challenges you foresaw," Petersen conceded, his voice laced with regret. "The rest are enduring pitiable conditions, secluded two hundred miles south, in a place known as Anoatuk."

"Torn by differing opinions, with sustenance dwindling," added Bonsall, his eyes shadowed with worry.

"They must be rescued at once!" Kane declared.

"Given the escalating number of ailing men, Mr. McGary, you must go. We have to rely on the assistance of these Esquimaux to transport the essential supplies and bring back our comrades."

McGary nodded, understanding the urgency. "I'll leave immediately."

As Kane and McGary immersed themselves in organizing relief provisions, Petersen looked at them with a glint of gratitude. "Your goodwill is highly commendable," he said.

"Your courage in returning could be their salvation," Kane responded earnestly.

A week later, inside the icy confines of the brig, Kane and his crew were enveloped in slumber when the vigilant Brooks raised an alarm.

"Captain, Esquimaux approaching," Brooks announced urgently.

Kane bundled up and navigated through the igloo's constricted entryway without wasting a moment.

Once on the deck, enveloped in darkness, it took Kane a moment to discern their returning mates, their identities concealed behind the native attire. Accompanied by Esquimaux with their formidable and healthy dog teams, McGary returned, his sledge worn, his dogs exhausted. The invalids were packed on the sledges, wrapped in furs, their faces etched with hunger and encrusted with frost and snow.

Each man ascending the gangway was met with a hearty handshake or a comforting pat from Kane, his eyes brimming with relief and gratitude. Kane warmly welcomed Godfrey, whose embarrassment radiated from every aspect of his demeanor. Spotting Dr. Hayes, the last man, with a pronounced limp, Kane hastened to his aid.

"Fortunate to have you back in one piece," Kane declared, his voice carrying a note of profound relief.

"By a hair's breadth," responded Hayes, his voice barely above a whisper.

"It's consoling to be back on familiar grounds."

The men quickly settled in, savoring generous servings of coffee, meat-biscuit soup, molasses, wheat bread, and salt pork, all while sharing their harrowing tales. The six Esquimaux also nestled across the buffalo skin beside the stove.

Shunghu

"These chiefs are Kaluntah and Shunghu," Petersen introduced with a nod from each man, marking his introduction.

"Our sustenance for the past two months was frozen seal and walrus meat at a site known as Peteravik," revealed Hayes.

"Every abode we encountered on our return granted us nourishment, rest, and a moment to dry and warm, no questions asked," added Petersen.

McGary gifted each rescuer needles, a file, and a wooden stick, with Kaluntah and Shunghu receiving hunting knives.

"We had to take some fox skins and sundries from them during our journey," admitted Hayes.

"Convey our intentions of returning the borrowed items to them," Kane instructed Petersen.

Spirited and content, the Esquimaux returned to their homes with their newfound treasures.

"I presume we are overlooking the knives and forks that just vanished?" queried Petersen as they departed.

"Consider them borrowed," replied Kane as he scrutinized Dr. Hayes's foot, revealing alarming frostbite and exposed bones due to scurvy.

"Your foot is in dire need of care, Dr. Hayes," stated Kane earnestly. "While I attend to this, Mr. Petersen, would you arrange to clear some space outside for our expanded company?"

"Indeed, sir," agreed Petersen. "And given it's Christmas, having the entire crew present will make it merrier."

The following evening, inside the brig, the crew assembled to commemorate Christmas with a special dinner, immersed in camaraderie and momentarily casting aside their present afflictions and bygone disagreements.

"Gentlemen," began Kane, "I vow to you all on this joyful day. No matter the challenges, next Christmas shall find you amidst the warmth of your homes."

A resounding cheer filled the room.

"To accompany this pledge, I have a modest indulgence," Kane continued. "Tom, pass around the remaining sillery."

Tom Hickey fetched the bottle from Kane's locker, allocating a modest portion for each man.

"It may have lost its vibrancy, yet it remains unmatched… for it is the last of its kind," commented Hickey.

"I dedicate this toast to my faraway family and friends," shared Brooks.

"My perception alters not the meal, but its essence, not as pork and beans, but as sumptuous roast turkey adorned with onions," mused Wilson.

"I visualize mine as succulent boiled roast beef, partnered with potatoes and cucumbers," injected Ohlsen.

"Yes, cucumbers and strawberries," Hickey concurred. While joy filled the air, in a quiet corner, Godfrey discreetly enveloped some pork pieces with bread in a soiled handkerchief and concealed it in his pocket.

"I yearn for melon," proclaimed Morton. "Let's unveil the reserves!"

Struggling to mask his paleness and evident malaise. McGary endeavored to immerse himself in the day's festive spirit. "Ain't got no 'reserve!'"

"Then bring on the beans!" Morton shouted.

The men ate, laughed, and sang shanty songs inside their cozy home.

Days later, in the brig's igloo, Dr. Hayes, perspiring from pain and fever, stifled his groans but could not disguise the tears in his eyes. McGary was bedridden. Mr. Ohlsen collapsed when he last crossed the living area. Hickey tried to stop his fall, but he also collapsed. Only Kane, Hans, Petersen, Brooks, and Bonsall were fit enough to help the others.

"After their ordeal, when the time comes, it may be hard to get the men who had been gone to leave the security of the ship again," Brooks said. "When the time comes, I doubt there'll be a choice," Kane said.

Petersen came to Kane from the direction of Dr. Hayes' bed.

"Dr. Hayes has fallen unconscious," relayed Petersen with a sense of urgency in his voice.

"The agony seems to have overwhelmed him again. It might be prudent for you to examine him, sir."

With hastened steps, Kane went to Hayes' bedside and gently began to unwind the bandages encircling his foot.

"I fear we may have no alternative but to amputate this foot," disclosed Kane, his voice strained with regret. "And I sincerely hope that will suffice."

With deliberate haste, Petersen retrieved the surgical instruments, filling a pan with chunks of ice and placing it over the stove to boil the water; the air filled with a tangible tension.

In the confines of the brig, Kane couldn't help but reflect on the audacity of performing such a critical surgery in their rudimentary and cluttered surroundings. The dim lighting and the limited space weighed heavily on his mind. Every incision and suture was a delicate balance between life and death, and the stakes were higher than ever in this unforgiving Arctic wilderness.

As they meticulously worked to save their crewmate, the enormity of their situation bore down on him, and he couldn't escape the thought that their struggle for survival was an unending battle against both the elements and the limitations of their makeshift medical bay.

XVIII. Point of No Return

Amid the cover of darkness on the deck, Kane scrubbed away the vestiges of the surgery, the tranquil whispers of the sleeping crew surrounding him. His body convulsing in illness and swaddled in layers, McGary kept a solemn vigil alongside him. Kane's focus sharpened as he strained to decipher the minute script on paper under the flickering lantern light.

"The vessel will lose her seaworthiness with the fuel we extract from the hull over the next thirty days," Kane's voice broke through the quiet, a shadow of despair creeping over his features. "Our only recourse now is to plan an escape across the formidable ice using the boats."

"The proposition seems insurmountable," McGary responded, his voice weary. "Our supplies of fresh food are depleted. Scurvy spreads its sinister grasp further. My breath grows scarce, and eruptions mar my skin. Not just scurvy but frostbite and other maladies. And a month of relentless winter still looms over us."

"We find ourselves in a relentless duel with a silent and unrelenting foe," Kane pronounced gravely. "Survival through this winter is uncertain, let alone the looming months that follow."

"Could hopes of a rescue expedition be plausible, akin to Franklin's?" inquired McGary.

"Would they risk another vessel and its loyal crew?" Kane mused, the rhetorical question hanging heavily in the air. "It seems a distant hope. Our liberation from this icy prison hinges on ourselves and on securing fresh provisions."

"Hans relentlessly scours the land daily, his efforts fruitless," McGary retorted, a sense of abandonment coloring his words. "This harsh second winter has torn the remnants of our nation's flag from our mast. It seems we are utterly forsaken."

"Our salvation rests upon the resilience of our spirits and our resourcefulness," Kane offered his words as a beacon of hope amidst despair. "We cannot afford the loss of another soul. We must unearth a remedy for this cursed scurvy."

The next evening, inside the brig, Kane, McGary, Bonsall, Petersen, and the afflicted who had the strength to sit were huddled around the stove. They sipped on one of Kane's concocted brews, expressions of distaste marking their faces.

"The blend of flaxseed and quinine rivals the most unpalatable concoctions you've dared to label as beer," McGary remarked with a grimace.

The entrance gave way to Hans, bearing three rabbits in his arms.

"A divine surprise!" exclaimed Kane, his voice a weak echo of joy. "Feed the blood to Ohlsen and Morton promptly and ensure full meat rations reach the bedridden. With luck, the sun should grace us with its presence soon."

Days later, while Hans is out hunting again, those with the strength to stand on the deck congregated, witnessing the first true sun rays drape the brig's deck in golden hues.

"We have languished so long in the shadowed abyss; to witness light once more feels akin to being bathed in celestial glory," Brooks mused.

"A spectacle of unparalleled radiance!" shouted Petersen, his voice filled with jubilance. "A vision of supreme splendor!"

"Ho!" Kane's yell cut through the air. "Is that the silhouette of Hans?"

"He hauls something on the sledge," noted Kane, his voice tinged with hopeful wonder. "Could it be?"

The men ambled with eager strides to greet Hans on the frosty terrain as he approached the brig, his meager two-dog sledge laden with a deer of inestimable worth.

"One more Tuk Tuk, dead, back in the ravine," Hans conveyed.

With waning strength, the men labored to unload the deer carcass, their movements strained and slow. The task of elevating it over the side sapped their remaining energy. Hans took his leave to retrieve the other deer while, on deck, the men grappled with the stiff, frozen carcass. The restricted hatchway compelled them to saw it into manageable pieces, their feeble arms moving with resurgent energy.

Inside the brig around midday, a week later, the scene was one of subdued activity. Kane shattered a large mirror into smaller fragments, gathering items that reflected light or were useful for mounting. Morton, hindered by a bad foot, chopped up frozen Manila hawsers for fuel, and Bonsall diligently chipped at ice sacks.

"In our reduced state, with only two of us to accomplish all tasks," Bonsall inquired, his breath forming misty clouds in the frigid air.

"It appears so," Kane conceded with a heavy heart. "Some show signs of recovery, while others continue to deteriorate."

"Dr. Hayes clings to life by sheer willpower alone," Bonsall remarked, his eyes filled with concern.

"The relentless advance of scurvy shows no mercy," Kane said, his voice tinged with gravitas. "Our efforts must become even more relentless."

As the daylight waned, Kane meticulously arranged a series of mirrors, making minute adjustments until a cascade of sunlight bathed the dim room. He skillfully manipulated the mirrors to cast beams of light upon the afflicted crew members, eliciting feeble smiles from those who still had the strength to respond. Meanwhile, Bonsall carefully relocated Riley to a less damp bunk.

Riley's protests echoed in the close confines of the brig. "Where am I being taken?" he inquired.

With a hint of resignation in his voice, Petersen delivered the grim news. "Our meat reserves have been depleted once again."

A shadow of fear crossed Riley's face as he contemplated the unthinkable sacrifice that might be required to sustain them.

"We must procure meat," Kane declared with unwavering determination. Turning to Hans, he issued a directive. "Hans, venture south and seek assistance from the Esquimaux. Use their dogs to hunt walrus. I will scour the northern terrains in search of sustenance."

Hans nodded in agreement, accepting the challenging task.

A week passed, and within the confines of the brig, Kane devoted himself to chronicling their arduous journey in his journal. Godfrey, showing signs of recovery, diligently fashioned a boot from deerskin. Faint sounds of dogs and subtle commotions on the deck signaled Hans' return. He entered, carrying Kane's Marston rifle.

Kane's somber admission filled the room. "My efforts yielded no results. What about you?"

Hans conveyed the grim situation. "The Etah people have no food. They have resorted to eating their dogs. They will not hunt until they see the Marston shoot. I managed to procure a small walrus with Myouk's help."

Kane's resolve remained unshaken. "You must continue hunting with Myouk."

As if on cue, Myouk, his emaciated frame testifying to their dire circumstances, entered the room, bearing precious meat. Despite his weakened state, he managed a playful tweak at Kane's cheek before depositing his burden, collapsing into a deep slumber.

"We must make this meat last longer," Kane contemplated aloud. "We will prepare broths and allocate scant portions solely to the ailing, once daily."

Bonsall interjected with a chilling reminder of their harsh reality. "The temperature is fifty-two below, and today, we burned the last strand of the Manila hawser."

Kane made a determined decision. "We have no choice but to burn the trebling. It may not save the ship, but it will keep us alive until summer."

In frustration, Godfrey abandoned his boot project and stormed out, dismay echoing in the confined space. "You've doomed her, along with all remaining hope!"

A heavy silence settled in the room as Kane and the others absorbed the weight of his words.

"Hans, you will return to Etah tomorrow," Kane instructed, his voice unwavering. "Take the Sharpes with you and leave the Marston here. Your hunting skills are needed more than ever."

In Kane's mind, the path to their salvation was clear: the rejuvenation of their health through consuming fresh meat.

Weeks trudged by, and the team's hunting achievements remained marginal, though sufficient to sustain their fragile state.

XIX. Theft & Escape

In the quiet, dim corners of the brig, where the howling winds outside whispered secrets of impending doom, Stevenson cautiously woke Kane. His hand hovered in the air momentarily before gently shaking Kane's shoulder.

"Godfrey," Stevenson whispered, his voice barely audible, "he approached me, urging me to join his escape plan come morning. I declined, but I suspect Wilson might be swayed despite his supposedly worsening condition."

Kane's brow furrowed as he absorbed the news. He knew that any attempt to leave the brig in its current state could have dire consequences.

Kane, unable to sleep, decided to confront Godfrey first. He needed to gauge the depth of Godfrey's desperation and ensure the crew's unity.

"It's your turn to prepare the morning meal," Kane declared, his gaze fixed intently on Godfrey's every move. Godfrey, visibly distressed, reluctantly rose from his bunk. He exchanged furtive whispers with Wilson, whose once-sturdy demeanor had crumbled with each passing day.

As the crew began to stir and the specter of a potential escape loomed in the air, Kane knew he had to act swiftly. He couldn't allow dissent to fracture their already fragile group further.

"Bonsall, Morton," Kane announced, his voice echoing through the dimly lit space, "I require your assistance this morning for our routine tasks outside."

Tension mounted as the crew members exchanged wary glances, sensing something was amiss. They had been teetering on the brink of survival for too long, and desperation was a dangerous catalyst.

After a meager breakfast, Kane donned his fur-lined garments, concealing a revolver beneath them. Bonsall and Morton, also prepared for their assigned tasks, exchanged uneasy glances, unsure of what the day would bring.

"We'll be heading over to the island for our daily readings," Kane proclaimed for all to hear.

Outside the igloo but still within the confines of the brig, Kane huddled Bonsall and Morton together. The gravity of their situation hung heavy in the frigid air.

"We can't afford any disruptions," Kane whispered urgently. "Stay vigilant and be prepared for anything. You two head above, making some noise, and be prepared to return quickly."

With the dread mounting, the crew's fate hung in the balance, their struggles against the unforgiving Arctic wilderness pushing them to the brink of despair. The darkness outside mirrored the uncertainty within as they braced themselves for the challenges ahead.

Kane moved swiftly and silently, slipping into a shadowy corner by the igloo's entrance. He listened intently as Bonsall and Morton clamored their way up above. Time seemed to stretch on as Kane held his breath, concealed in the darkness. Eventually, Wilson emerged with his limp mysteriously absent, making his way up the ladder.

Moments later, Godfrey emerged, dressed for travel and wrapped in buffalo skins. He went over to a pile of sail material and retrieved a sack of stolen supplies from underneath it. As soon as Godfrey had them in hand, Kane stepped out from his dark hiding place, revolver drawn.

"Your treacherous plans are laid bare, Godfrey," Kane declared with a steely gaze. "Back inside."

Godfrey shook his head in disgust, and a moment later, Wilson descended the steps with Bonsall and Morton following, sidearms drawn. Wilson's limp returned as quickly as it had vanished, becoming more exaggerated as he locked eyes with Kane.

"Take them in," Kane ordered. "Shackle them and put them in the hold. Their fate will be settled in due course."

Igloo at Etah

Hans approached Shunghu's humble abode with cautious yet determined steps, a haven amidst the harsh Arctic surroundings. As he entered, the interior was a hive of activity. Shunghu reclined, his weathered face bearing the marks of countless hunts and trials, while his wife and two teenage daughters toiled tirelessly, their nimble fingers weaving the threads of survival - sewing furs, cooking, and mending dog harnesses, the lifelines of their arctic existence.

In the familiar cadence of their native tongue, Hans spoke with the gravity of their dire situation. "Shunghu, will you join me on a hunt?" he inquired, his voice quivering with anticipation.

Shunghu replied in kind, his eyes reflecting the harsh reality of their circumstances. "We, too, are in dire need of food," he spoke in Esquimaux, the urgency evident in his tone. "At dawn, we go."

Hans, eyes roving through the bustling room, encountered the gaze of the younger daughter. Her countenance, framed by the flickering light of a nearby oil lamp, betrayed a hint of vulnerability. A rosy blush graced her cheeks as their eyes briefly locked, and she quickly averted her gaze, her shyness a poignant contrast to the rugged environment that enveloped them.

As night drew on, Hans settled into the warmth of Shunghu's dwelling, mindful that their fortunes were now bound to the same hazardous venture. One of the daughters, her reserve worn away, brought him a bowl of food and spread furs for his bed. In these small courtesies lay a shared resolve, for the hunt at dawn would decide not only their survival, but that of those left aboard the icebound ship.

Back at the brig, the oppressive darkness with its uncomfortable silence hung heavy in the air, broken only by eerie creaks and groans of the ship. The anxiety in the room was again suffocating, especially for Godfrey and Wilson, their wrists chafing from the shackles that bound them. Morton's stern gaze remained fixed upon the two culprits, adding to the atmosphere of unease that pervaded every corner.

Kane, with focused diligence, sat hunched over the ship's log, methodically recording the acts of betrayal committed by Godfrey and Wilson. The weight of their theft and desertion was now etched into the official records of the expedition.

"Your theft and desertion are now official records," Kane stated, his voice cutting through the heavy silence. He looked at the two prisoners expectantly. "Have you anything to declare?"

Wilson attempted to speak, but his words barely formed before Godfrey's sharp interruption seized everyone's attention.

"I have plenty to declare!" Godfrey's voice was filled with a volatile mixture of rage and despair. "You murdered her."

Confusion clouded Morton's features. "What are you talking about?"

"My ship, you fool!" Godfrey's roar reverberated through the dimly lit room. "My destiny! My solitary chance to claim a captain's title is obliterated!"

Bonsall couldn't hide his incredulity. "Your ship?"

Kane, reluctantly impressed by Godfrey's revelation, confirmed it with a somber nod. "Yes, he was the prospective captain of the Advance."

"Yes," Godfrey gritted his teeth. "And you, with your ineptitude, doomed her. You encased her in the ice and methodically reduced her to mere kindling. She's undone. Our continued presence here is futile."

"The Fates left us no alternative," Kane defended, his voice both defiant and resolute.

"Under my command, such calamity would have been averted!" Godfrey's gaze bore into Kane's, a challenge in his eyes.

After a moment of tense silence, Kane decided. With measured reluctance, he reached for the keys to Godfrey's shackles, unlocking the restraints one by one. The clinks of the unlocking chains echoed through the room, serving as a haunting reminder of the unresolved conflicts that lingered.

"Upon our return, a formal hearing will be held," Kane declared, his voice reflecting his stoic resolution. "Restraining and guarding you here is impractical."

The shadows in the brig seemed to deepen as the weight of their uncertain future settled upon the group.

"So, I am free to leave?" Godfrey's question hung in the air, a spark of hopeful defiance gleaming in his eyes.

"No," Kane replied, steady and unyielding. "If you leave us again, you'll have no further aid from us. And should you steal, you will answer for it with your life."

"That will not happen," Godfrey said, his voice a blend of scorn and resignation.

Kane's voice broke the silence. "Report to Mr. Petersen," he ordered, the weight of command in every word. "You and Wilson will remove and cut the trebling."

In response, Godfrey met his gaze, the look between them charged with unspoken hostility.

At around the same time, exhausted from hunting and ailing, Hans and Shunghu battled the harsh blizzard as they stumbled back to Shunghu's hut in Etah. Rushing to their aid, Shunghu's wife and two daughters secured the dogs and helped the two men into the warmth of the hut.

Inside, the men lay shivering on the family's fur-covered platform and communal bed. Shunghu's wife attended to her husband while the younger daughter cared for Hans. The older daughter served hot soup from the kettle hanging over the fire. She held the bowl to Hans' lips with gentle hands, offering him comfort in his weakened state.

As dawn timidly bathed the brig in its feeble light, Petersen burst through the doorway, his breath coming in ragged spurts. Frustration and concern were etched across his features as he exclaimed, "I merely looked away for an instant, and Godfrey seized the opportunity to flee. He's abandoned his post once again."

Kane's expression hardened as he muttered, "Incorrigible. Did Wilson go with him?"

"No," Petersen replied sharply. "He remains hard at work."

"And the supplies?" questioned Kane, his brow furrowed.

"The very sack we confiscated," Petersen said, unease in his voice.

"He's headed for Etah with intentions to steal our sledge and dogs from Hans," deduced Kane, his eyes narrowing.

"If he succeeds, our situation will be far more perilous," Petersen replied, his words hanging heavily in the tense air.

Hans had taken ill for a time, but with the nursing by Shunghu's youngest, he had rapidly recovered. Within the cozy confines of his hut, the day after his recovery, Hans found comfort beneath fur covers, accompanied by Shunghu's younger daughter. Shunghu, his wife, and their eldest daughter were elsewhere, immersed in the pursuit of game.

"Remain with me," Shunghu's daughter pleaded in her native tongue.

"I have duties," responded Hans, also in Esquimaux. "I must hunt meat for my comrades."

"They will get other meat," she countered softly. "Stay with me."

Hans silently weighed her earnest plea until, with visible reluctance, he arose to depart.

"I shall come back," he promised, a blend of assurance and resolve in his gaze.

Stepping outside the shelter of the hut, Hans moved to retrieve his sledge and dogs, only to find them missing. A frown of puzzlement creased his brow as he surveyed the emptiness. With resolve and a hint of uncertainty shadowing his steps, he set forth northward, traversing the terrain on foot.

Two days later, Bonsall, his grip firm on the Marston rifle, hastened up the gangplank, his breaths coming in rapid, uneven gasps. Kane stood poised on the deck, a concealed pistol in his pocket.

"There's a man on the icefoot, roughly a mile distant," Bonsall reported, his eyes aflame with alertness. "I am not in his sight, I believe."

"That may be Godfrey. I'm going after him," Kane declared decisively. "He's after our supplies. Rouse the others."

On the ice, Kane drew his pistol as he approached the man, he believed was Godfrey. The man saw him, turned, abandoned his sledge and dogs, and fled south.

The man ran in a zigzag between the hummocks, gaining ground before stopping to hide behind a large one. He crouched against a smaller drift-covered mound to lower his profile—when a pair of paws appeared at its crest.

Kane, having lost sight of him, halted and listened. A polar bear vaulted over the hummock and lunged. The man sprang aside, barely beyond its reach, but the beast was on him in an instant, dragging him down in a furious struggle for life.

Kane heard the bear's thunderous roar, swiftly drew his pistol, and plunged through the hummocks toward the sounds of the relentless struggle.

Kane arrived to find a violent tangle of fur and parka rolling across the ice. He stopped, narrowing his eyes to make out the man beneath the bear. It was Godfrey. Kane hesitated, his thoughts racing. Godfrey's eyes met his—wide with fear, and aware of the pause in Kane's resolve.

With a resolve, Kane shot his pistol into the air. The loud bang startled the bear, causing it to flee, leaving Godfrey scratched but largely unscathed. Kane stood still, offering no hand to help Godfrey up.

"You were going to let him have me, weren't you?" Godfrey questioned, a mix of resentment and realization in his eyes.

Kane's expression gave nothing away. He only motioned with his pistol toward the stolen sledge.

Reaching the sledge, Kane prodded Godfrey to move ahead.

"Prepare the dogs," commanded Kane, his voice firm.

With a mix of reluctance and resignation, Godfrey complied.

"I had no intention of taking supplies," Godfrey insisted.

"Your deceit is continual," Kane retorted sharply. "You absconded with the sledge and dogs."

Godfrey stumbled as he adjusted a harness, then jogged beside the team on the way back to the brig.

"Hans is sick in Etah," he said, an edge of accusation in his voice.

"Once you are secured, I will find him," Kane answered, his gaze fixed on Godfrey. "If your actions have brought him harm, you will answer for it."

Beside the brig, Bonsall stood on the ice with the Marston leveled at Godfrey.

"Keep a close watch on him," Kane instructed. "I'm heading below to fetch the irons. When I see him next, I'll tell Hans about the bear."

Kane's abrupt return to the deck momentarily diverted Bonsall's attention, affording Godfrey a fleeting opportunity to wrest the Marston from Bonsall's grip and abscond again. Bonsall swiftly drew his pistol and pulled the trigger, but it malfunctioned at the cap.

In haste, Kane lunged for the gun rack, but the first rifle he seized misfired due to the cold while cocking.

Without a pause, Kane grasped another and rushed down the gangplank. Despite being at a long yet feasible distance, the hastily aimed second rifle failed to find its mark on the runaway. Once again, Godfrey had slipped away.

"Blast it!" Kane exclaimed. "The Marston is vital for our hunting—and may be our only chance of leaving this place."

"I regret it," Bonsall said, his voice low. "I'll go after him."

"Not while he holds the upper hand," Kane asserted, his voice firm yet edged with concern.

"He may return for more ammunition," Bonsall remarked, a firm resolve shadowing his eyes. "He only has a single round. I give you my word that he will not take me by surprise again."

With a sober glance, Kane inspected the meat Godfrey had left on the sledge.

The mood thickened as Kane and his crew faced the unsettling realization that their chances of survival were dwindling fast, and their treacherous crewmate remained at large, lurking in the unforgiving Arctic wilderness.

Within the confines of the brig that evening, Kane, with a passing gaze at Wilson—who reciprocated with a lowered head—addressed the entire crew.

"Given Godfrey's liberty, each of us is in danger," Kane declared, pacing rhythmically as he meticulously chose his words. "I'm compelled to assert that any subsequent endangerment to our welfare by anyone will be confronted immediately with the most severe consequences—death."

Bonsall drew Kane aside. "I must fetch Hans," he said. "My duty to him compels it."

"No," Kane replied. "I will find him, then pursue Godfrey to reclaim the Marston. Help me make ready."

Unexpectedly, Hans appeared.

"What delayed you?" inquired Kane.

"I was unwell," Hans answered. "Shunghu's younger daughter tended me." A faint smile crossed his face.

"For so long?" Kane pressed. "Did you see Godfrey?"

"Yes. He wished me to go south with him, but I refused. He wanted meat. I wished him gone, so I gave it."

"That's the meat we found on the sledge," Kane said. "Did you see him again?"

"Yes," Hans said. "He passed me on his way to Etah. He had Marston."

"We may be better without him," Kane said gravely, "yet he remains a danger. That rifle must be recovered. Hans, when you are strong enough, go straight to Cape Alexander and ask Kalutunah for four dogs."

Days later, while Kane diligently prepared his sledge and harnessed his rested dogs, Metek and Paulik arrived with a sledge and four resilient dogs. Frost enveloped them from crown to sole, yet their spirits were high, laughter echoing. McGary extended a pair of ankle-cuffs towards Kane, destined to be packed onto his sledge. With an aura of staunch vigilance, Kane inspected his revolver meticulously.

"McGary, ask Metek to go with me to Etah," instructed Kane, his voice steady.

McGary approached the laughing pair and gave the message. Metek cast Kane a solemn glance, then laughed all the louder and agreed. Paulik, however, was told to remain. Kane's likeness to the Esquimaux had grown so marked he might have been mistaken for Paulik himself.

"It is remarkable," McGary said, with a touch of wonder. "Even in the worst weather, the Esquimaux keep their laughter."

"Amazing," McGary agreed. "Facing the harshest conditions, Esquimaux just laugh."

Kane released a hearty laugh, his face breaking into a smile. "Their spirit is quite a contrast to ours. Well, Metek, it's time to go."

Kane pulled away. Watching him depart, a sudden wave of cramps seized McGary, causing him to double over in pain, his hand clutching his stomach. Paulik, with quick concern, assisted him inside.

Days later, Metek and Kane neared the settlement amidst the swirling blizzard. Despite the tempest, the villagers, a small assembly of enduring souls, poured forth to welcome back their chief. Etah, a modest congregation of shadowed huts, lay as mere smudges against the expansive snow drift, clung to the steep mountain flank. The dwellings seemed to blend into the land, like blemishes on the pristine white canvas of the relentless landscape.

Among the first of the welcoming crowd, with vigorous waves and vibrant chants of the Esquimaux greeting, "Tima," resounding as fervently as any native, was Godfrey. Unbeknownst to him, due to the obscuring snow flurry, he was unaware of the identity of his companion.

Kane, moving with the ease of one accustomed to the locals' ways, came upon him unannounced, breaking the silence with a low murmur: "Mr. Godfrey, I presume," he said, pressing the cold muzzle of a pistol to his ribs.

"Not again!" Godfrey's voice cracked with frustration. "Damn it! Why should you care whether I perish with you or with these Esquimaux?"

"I care only that you take no one else with you," Kane replied, his gaze fixed and unwavering.

"You're here for the Marston," Godfrey surmised, his voice a mix of resignation and subtle defiance.

"That's correct," Kane replied, his words steady yet loaded. "And to ensure you don't interfere further with our plans."

Godfrey's feet shuffled on the ground, eyes directed downwards, in contemplation or surrender. "I thought I could . . .

become a captain here— of this pack of natives," Godfrey said. "But after trying just a few days, I realize that'll never be. I realize now they can't be led."

"Why such an obsession with becoming a captain?" Kane asked, his brow lifting slightly.

"To follow my father's path—to command a ship, to be remembered," Godfrey replied. "But it is too late now."

"To be remembered for what?" Kane said. "A title alone? It is not rank that endures, but the deeds we render and the help we give our fellows."

"Like the Esquimaux do for each other, as I have learned?" Godfrey's words bore an edge. "Does your charity extend to me? Can I return? This land offers me nothing."

"You return only to confinement," Kane retorted. "We'll leave you here when we leave, when we pass back this way. You are not trusted, and you waste our precious time."

Godfrey's head bowed, his silence speaking of his resignation and acceptance. Kane's pistol guided Godfrey towards the huts. "That's unnecessary," Godfrey remarked. "I'm resigned to rejoin."

"The location of the Marston?" Kane probed sharply.

Venturing into one of the huts, they were met with salutations of "Nalegak" by its dwellers. The Marston rifle lay inconspicuously against the wall. Swiftly, Kane disarmed it, the lone cartridge disappearing into his pocket. Two small stoves burned with the smoky fuel of walrus oil, their small flames casting an ambient flicker around the room.

Chains clinked as Kane snapped them around Godfrey's ankles. Kane then nestled himself amongst the furs next to the semi-circular sleeping platform. Kane mingled with the lively, well-nourished, untidy, undraped co-inhabitants. The overwhelming heat and the throng of individuals provoked Kane to assimilate into the mixture of natives, each enveloped in their layer of grime. They interwove like entangled worms in a bait container.

The acceptance of filth was plain enough. A woman prodded old bones and refuse beneath the sleeping platform with a stick, sending a scatter of puppies into the open. Metek and his wife worked at the walrus flipper, great mouthfuls vanishing into Metek's distended cheeks before being neatly severed and swallowed.

He offered Kane a piece, which Kane declined, as he did Godfrey's frozen liver. A moment later, he reconsidered, taking the flipper and eating with the others. The rough fellowship of the meal was a mingling of closeness and distance.

He then cast his weary form across the limbs of Mrs. Eider-Duck, who gently nestled her plump infant in the crook of his arm. Kane rested his head against the comforting warmth of the woman's abdomen and succumbed to slumber.

As the morning light pierced the slumber, Kane awoke to find Godfrey awake, sitting, and eating. Mrs. Eider-Duck had prepared breakfast, and as Kane rose and dressed, she extended a piece of boiled blubber, and a prime cut of meat served on a curved bone. Accepting the chunk of meat without the bone, Kane finished dressing, released Godfrey's ankle irons, grabbed the Marston, and nudged Godfrey to his feet and toward the entrance, taking bites of his meat as they moved.

"Before we set out, I must speak with Awahtok," Kane said, tossing the irons onto the sledge.

"The chief's hut is next door," Godfrey said.

Within the chief's hut, Awahtok, alongside two venerable elders, reclined on furs. Awahtok, his toes marked with the darkness of healing frostbite, nursed his extremities carefully.

"Ulaakut," Kane voiced, employing the Esquimaux tongue for 'good morning,' his proficiency gradually growing with each interaction.

Acknowledgments came in the form of silent nods from Awahtok, Angekok—the village seer—and Ootuniah.

"How far lies the open water, and is it drawing nearer?" Kane asked in the Esquimaux tongue.

"Beyond the cape," Awahtok replied, his words in their native speech, "it comes about an hour's walk toward Etah in the space of one moon.

"By the heavens!" Kane exclaimed. "That equates to four miles in merely four weeks. Our journey will require hauling boats over one hundred and forty icy miles to reach open waters. I'd hoped for half of that."

"You can't move loaded boats a hundred and forty miles over ice," Godfrey said.

Kane, his focus unwavering, afforded him no response. "Can we use your dogs to help us move from the ship to open water?" Kane asked in Esquimaux.

Awahtok looked at Angekok, who shook his head.

"They are with Kalutunah," Awahtok said.

As Kane started to ask where Kalutunah was, Hans entered.

"Mr. Brooks sent me to get you," Hans said. "Mr. McGary is worse."

"We must leave," Kane said in Esquimaux. "Thank you for your help and the walrus meat. Let's go."

"I'm ready," Godfrey said.

The Esquimaux stepped outside to see Kane off.

"Hans, find Kalutunah and tell him to meet us at the brig," Kane said. "Let him know that, in exchange for his help with the sledges and dogs, we'll give him the Capstan bar to make his harpoons."

Hans set off south, and Kane and Godfrey went north, dragging a hefty load of meat with only four dogs. Kane pushed the sledge, and

Godfrey pulled it, stumbling beside it and sometimes adjusting the load.

When they arrived at the brig, the rest of the crew was still asleep, except for Goodfellow, who was on watch. Kane pulled out the ankle-irons from the sledge to put on Godfrey. "You don't need those," Godfrey said. "I've accepted my fate."

"If you cross me again…" Kane said, his voice firm.

"I know," Godfrey said, his voice steady. "It won't happen."

Acknowledging their dire straits and the pressing circumstances, Kane felt a tight knot of urgency in his chest; it was time to rally the men and leave, and any delay could spell peril for them all.

XX. Food & Message

That night, within the confines of the brig, Kane positioned himself near the stove, a solitary figure amongst the slumbering men—save for Brooks.

"Time is running thin," remarked Brooks, his tone somber. He glanced at the dimly lit bottle of brandy on a nearby shelf, a twenty-five-year-old promise for finding Franklin. "Seems we may never lay eyes on that bottle."

"We are unprepared for the forthcoming trials," conceded Kane, his voice heavy with gravity. He looked over at McGary, whose trembling form lay shrouded in fever, allowing delirium to pierce his moments of lucidity.

The following morning, Kane and the others were still endeavoring to aid McGary, hindered by the absence of Dr. Hayes' skilled touch and vast experience. Dr. Hayes, shadowed by his lingering despondency, found the rising clamor inescapable. Eventually, the makeshift caregivers' clumsy attempts to tend to McGary reached a tipping point for him. Even in his bedridden state, he began to issue directives.

"Prepare a rudimentary concoction of Citrate and a tincture of chloro-hydrated iron," Hayes instructed, his voice weak yet steady. His eyes, though weary, held a spark of determination. "It's proven somewhat effective against the ravages of scurvy."

"We could blend it with brandy," suggested Kane, considering their available supplies. He gestured toward the bottle that had symbolized hope.

At this, Dr. Hayes elevated himself slightly in his bed, a flicker of curiosity in his eyes.

"I was under the impression we had exhausted our supply of spirits?" he inquired, a hint of surprise interwoven with his fatigue.

"We still possess a bottle of twenty-five-year-old brandy, reserved for the day we would find Franklin," Kane declared, his voice touched with a hint of melancholy. He retrieved the bottle, its glass cold to the touch, and placed it beside Hayes. "It seems there is no longer a need to preserve it."

"Ah, if only we had a box of Havanas," interjected Hayes, a faint spark of hope in his voice.

A murmur of agreement passed among the men, though they knew such a wish would remain unfulfilled as Kane produced the infamous bottle of whisky.

"Men," Kane said with measured gravity, "the hour has come to prove our resolve once more. At dawn, we depart."

The next morning, while the brandy did manage to lift their spirits, a somber mood still hung over the men. They exchanged knowing glances, their gaze lingering on the harsh reality surrounding them. The realization that abandoning the comparative safety of the brig would demand a fortitude hitherto unknown weighed heavily on their hearts.

The subsequent morning, inside the brig, buzzed with activity from all those capable. McGary, having overcome his crisis, now sat upright. Riley, Morton, and Bonsall were diligently dismantling the cabin bulkhead to retrieve a substantial crossbeam, meticulously and laboriously fashioning sledge runners from it.

With his heel nearing recovery, Morton fashioned bolts from curtain rods, seated and focused. Petersen sharpened tools for Ohlsen, his hands steady and methodical. Kane handed battered, rusted tins and a stove pipe to Ohlsen, his gaze stern yet hopeful. The air was dense with determination and silent resolve, a tacit understanding of the looming ordeal shared by each man present.

"Examine these; see if they can serve as mess gear," instructed Kane.

"It's heartening to see Dr. Hayes muster the strength to grace the deck with his presence, to absorb some light," Morton remarked.

 Kalutunah, a dignified figure with a significant presence, along with Shangtu and Tatterat, entered, their arms laden with walrus meat. Once the customary greetings were exchanged, Kalutunah positioned himself beside Kane.

"Hans succeeded in reaching you," noted Kane. "Invaluable assistance. Mr. Hickey, please fetch our finest provisions. Morton, could you procure some tokens of appreciation for our benevolent guests, the Capstan bar included?"

Morton returned promptly with the Capstan bar, a knife, and several needles. Kane presented them to Kalutunah with a nod of gratitude.

"Kuyanaka! Asakaoteet!" expressed Kalutunah.

"He extends his thanks and refers to you as a friend—or, more aptly, he declares his deep affection for you," translated McGary."

Kalutunah, with a hint of mystery, retrieved a letter concealed within his glove and extended it to Kane, leaving him taken aback, aware that the Esquimaux neither possessed paper nor the knowledge of script.

"It is Hans's old letter of promotion," Kane said, his brow knit in puzzlement. "What does it mean? Where is Hans?"

McGary put the questions to Kalutunah, who answered with a shrug—silence speaking more than words. Kane saw no further explanation would come.

"Men, the hour has come to load the boats," he said, turning to the work at hand.

The subsequent morning saw the deck of the brig buzzing with fervent activity as preparations were underway. Ohlsen busily fortified the boats, embedding oak pieces in the bottom and appending light cedar washboards around the gunwales to enhance buoyancy. With meticulous precision, McGary was draping lightweight canvas over the boats, ensuring it was taut against the sides, forming a partial refuge from the impending waves, while removable masts were placed in each vessel.

McGary and Bonsall were securing the "Red Eric" atop the ancient sledge as others assisted in loading it with essential wood for fuel. Each vessel's condition was precarious at best, far from seaworthy. Discovering separations between the boards of the "Faith," Ohlsen was quick to seal the gaps with oakum and pitch.

Mr. Sontag was delicately enclosing his chronometers and other pieces of equipment while Bonsall was diligently packing powder and shot, handing over the remaining invaluable percussion caps to Kane, who stored them securely in his pocket.

Petersen meticulously organized makeshift pots and cooking utensils within each boat, fashioned from stove pipes and tin remnants. Improvised plates were created from assorted tin cans, and some revealed their previous contents through faint labels, like "Borden's Meat-biscuits" or "Corrosive Sublimate and Arsenic."

The men were also industrious in fabricating necessities—canvas moccasins were crafted with seal hide soles, blankets were transfigured into garments, curtains were stitched into Eider-down quilts, and bags brimmed with ship bread were firmly secured. The tangible anticipation and the pressing need for readiness filled the air as each man focused on his task, knowing the journey ahead demanded their utmost resilience and preparedness.

XXI. Departure

After days of relentless labor, Kane called the men together. Once assembled, he announced with formality, "We are ready. According to my official directive, we depart tomorrow."

"In the remaining time, gather your personal belongings—but no more than eight pounds each," Brooks instructed.

The announcement sent waves of concern through the already morose and ailing crewmembers, their worries about safety and survival intensifying their despondence.

On the ice, the laden boats stood ready, and the strength of most men was summoned to inch the first one toward the icefoot. "It seems the boats will transition smoother than anticipated," observed Brooks.

"The supplies haven't been loaded yet," Kane pointed out.

"Nor the invalids," added Bonsall.

"We will send the sick ahead by sledge to Anoatuk," Kane said. "Once past that point, all will be moved on to Etah. Even so, the boats will bear a heavy weight."

Morale experienced a tentative uplift as the men watched the initial boat move.

Subsequently, the boats were stationed higher on the icefoot, fully equipped, mirroring the men's aspirations for their eventual encounter with open water.

The relentless Arctic gales had frayed the ship's original American flags into fragments. From his inner coat, McGary produced a makeshift American flag he had stitched from pieces of the cherished blue fabric adorned with little red roses from his wife's dress, employing the roses as stars. He proceeded to each boat, symbolically hoisting his handcrafted flag up and down each mast.

"This is it," McGary declared. "We're ready."

"Hickey has concocted a special meal for us, the finest our scant provisions can offer," announced Kane. "Tonight, we revel! I only wish I knew Hans's fate." He led the men below.

On their final night within the brig, the entire crew, save for Hans, congregated in the stripped-down winter chamber for a concluding farewell to their trusty abode.

"Should we go find Hans?" Brooks asked.

"Not at this time; I have a suspicion of where he is, and he knows how to survive in this environment," Kane said. "We won't worry unless we have a reason for concern."

The moss walls had been disassembled, the supporting timber repurposed for fuel, and their beds relocated to the boats, leaving behind a barren, chilly, and desolate shell. With their meal concluded, they huddled together. Brooks arose before the others.

"I've composed a letter," disclosed Brooks. "It enumerates the charges against Godfrey."

A low groan passed through the men—the thought of reopening half-healed wounds hung heavy, just as spirits had begun to lift. Brooks struck a match, touched it to the letter, and with the flame lit a candle. Cheers rose, and Godfrey offered Brooks a smile and a handshake. Silence returned as Kane, having earlier removed Sir Franklin's portrait, sealed it in India-rubber.

"The challenges we are about to face are undeniable," proclaimed Kane. "However, consider the many hardships we've endured; some invisible kindness has protected us. We fervently hope that this protective kindness stays with us."

That night, they reposed wherever their bedding lay—most within the boats, a few beneath the canvases on the deck.

The following day, the men congregated on the deck around Kane. He hoisted McGary's American flag up the brig's mast and lowered it for the last time, marking the final time the American flag would flutter above the Advance. The men meandered around the brig, examining her one last time, reminiscing about the origins of her scars, and voicing their mixed feelings about abandoning her. The remnants of moss walls, the copper pots now brimming with frozen water, the theodolite, the chart-box, Wilson's guitar, ineffective daguerreotypes, and, most heartbreakingly, the skeletal remains of animals and other gathered specimens were all tangible remnants of relentless labor.

Near the bow, on the ice, Morton, Godfrey, Sontag, and Ohlsen gazed at the figurehead, Augusta. She still resembled a little girl, clothed in blue, with rosy cheeks, despite losing a piece of her breast to an iceberg, a fragment of her nose to a nip, and having her paint faded and chipped. Kane approached them.

"We ought to take Augusta with us," Morton said.

"We can't afford the additional weight," retorted Kane.

"If she becomes too much, we can always use her for firewood," Godfrey interjected. "And if she makes it back, then so have we."

"Very well," consented Kane. "She's your responsibility. Place her on the Faith."

Invigorated, the men hastened to detach her from the brig.

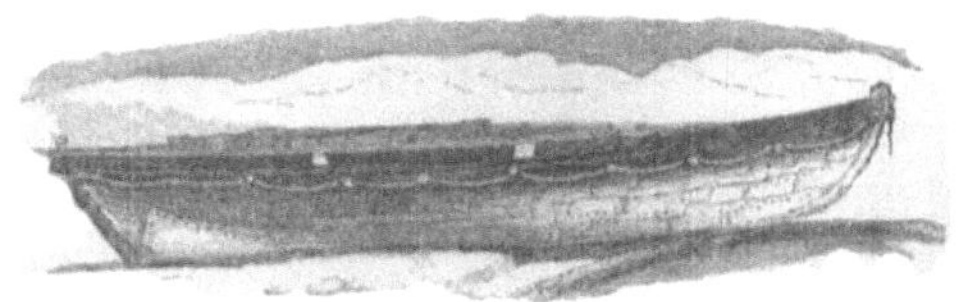

The Faith

The men meticulously inspected the boats, verifying their gear and ensuring readiness. Five men attempted to maneuver one of them, but it remained stationary.

"Listen up," directed Brooks. "We'll move one at a time."

"Mr. Brooks, you'll oversee the Red Eric," Kane announced. "Mr. Godfrey, the Faith. I'll take charge of the Hope. Put on your rue-raddies."

McGary exchanged a knowing wink with Kane, conscious of Kane's premeditated assignment of Godfrey to a boat. Brooks' contingent comprised Ohlsen, Mr. Bonsall, Petersen, and Hickey. Meanwhile, Godfrey was allocated a team including Mr. Sontag, Riley, Blake, and Morton. Kane's group included Goodfellow, Johannsen, Stevenson, and Parker. The ailing men in the group were Dr. Hayes, Wilson, and Whipple.

The hardy team members undertook the task of moving the first boat; a coordinated effort of pushing and pulling eventually set it in slow motion across the ice. During this concerted endeavor, a rat scurried away from the brig and leaped into the Faith, blending into the backdrop of men at work.

Moving the Ill

Kane and Goodfellow transported the ailing men to Anoatuk utilizing a sledge the following day. They settled them within a deserted, low-ceilinged hut. Given the hut's dimness, a lamp was also placed to provide illumination, and they were enshrouded with furs for warmth. Dr. Hayes, grappling with a wooden and leather prosthesis in place of his absent foot, found maintaining his position on the sledge challenging. Concurrently, both Wilson and Whipple were embroiled in their respective battles against the ravages of scurvy.

Four nights later, on the ice, Kane and Brooks sat atop kegs around a small stove, a coffee pot sending up fragrant steam. Only two of the three boats were there; the Red Eric still lay at the brig, its outline faint in the distant haze.

"Seven miles in four days," commented Brooks with a hint of displeasure, "It's not the progress we envisioned or need to make."

"Nonetheless, the shifting landscape provides a welcome balm to our spirits," Kane optimistically retorted.

"The 'Eric' is next to be moved," stated Brooks. "The heavier work has sharpened the men's appetites."

"We'll increase the bread ration tomorrow," declared Kane, his voice carrying a tone of resolve.

Upon returning from the brig, where Hickey had assumed the responsibilities of cook and baker, Kane felt a sting of sorrow observing the men's wearied movements. Brooks' legs, swollen and strained, tautly filled his trousers. Unpacking a batch of freshly baked bread, Kane distributed loaves to men and dogs, along with dried beans and apples.

"A trifle impaired, but still fit to eat," Kane remarked, examining the dried apples and beans.

"Good enough," Brooks replied, "but we need fresh meat to ward off scurvy. We've scarcely gained a mile since yesterday."

"I share your concerns regarding the ill we relocated to Anoatuk," Kane conceded. "They, too, need this bread. Afterward, I'll attempt to procure some walrus at Etah."

Kane disseminated food while navigating through the men dispersed along the ice floes.

A relentless blizzard greeted Kane, Morton, and Godfrey on the subsequent night at Anoatuk. Snow accumulated vehemently against the entrance of the hut. Hastily, Kane unloaded sustenance, fuel, and sleeping bags onto the snow before Godfrey departed.

"I'll make haste to Etah to secure meat," Godfrey informed.

"Do not linger," Kane replied. "Take what they can spare and bring it straight to the boats. Leave some here, and when you pass the sick, judge their condition. Make all speed."

The unhinged, crude doorway opened to reveal a darkness within the hut, starkly contrasting with the perpetual daylight outside. Within the hut, the sick men were in alarming condition, almost in delirium. They had been left in shadows, their lamp extinguished for days, and their sustenance depleted.

Morton and Kane worked quickly, opening the roof vent for fresh air and kindling a fire in the pit with tarred rope. They set the damp bedding to dry, moved the sick nearer the warmth, and prepared a broth of meat-biscuit and peas. The crumbling doorway was shored up, and a strip of rancid smoked pork was hung by the flame, its drippings feeding the lamp.

In the glow of renewed warmth and light, the afflicted found brief respite from their suffering. Satisfied they were as comfortable as possible, Kane and Morton returned to the boats.

Several days later, Godfrey returned with Metek, Nalegak, and another sledge, bringing a generous supply of walrus meat for the crew moving the boats along the ice. They stopped briefly at the hut to leave provisions for the sick, then proceeded to the boats to distribute the remaining load among the men.

Godfrey, Metek, and Nalegak reached the boats, where the party marked a modest gain—ten miles advanced. Though their feet were swollen and their bodies worn, their spirits held.

"Fourteen hours labor, and we've only moved one and a half miles from the brig since yesterday, covering a surface of twelve miles," commented Brooks.

"Slow work, but in the right direction," replied Kane. "We'll stop here and feed the men." "Meat—our tonic," Brooks declared.

By the ensuing morning, the plentiful meat supply had revitalized the men. The Faith, now being towed, maintained a steady pace. McGary and Hayes, who adapted to a homemade crutch in place of his absent foot, bid farewell to Kane as he embarked to procure more sustenance and facilitate their upcoming arrival at Etah.

"Vigilance!" McGary shouted. "The ice looks leaden—likely soft beneath."

"Exercise caution," warned Kane. "Even a trivial gale could transform this fragile ice field into a chaotic icepack."

"We're in the process of relocating the provisions from the ice," informed Brooks.

"Excellent," replied Kane. "Proceed towards Point Refuge on Littleton Island. I will meet you there. Petersen and I are bound for Etah to uncover Hans' fate."

"As you pass Anoatuk, tell the incapacitated to be ready to move," advised Hayes.

Acknowledging with a nod, Kane withdrew to ready a sledge for the southward journey. He felt relief, knowing the boats and men were in motion, even though a daunting thousand miles lay between them and sanctuary.

XXII. Final Journey to Etah

Several nights later, under the faint illumination of a waning crescent moon, Kane and Petersen found themselves nearing the Etah cape. The distant echoes of laughter and lively chatter traveled across the icy stretch, starkly contrasting the solemn quietude of the frozen land. It was as if life itself had concentrated in this small enclave of humanity amidst the vast, indifferent wilderness.

Before them, around thirty inhabitants—men, women, and children—rested on a rise of rock strewn with the traces of daily life, just beyond their village. The huts, weathered by years and storms, stood as mute witnesses to many seasons of hardship and reprieve.

Uncertainty stirred in Kane once more. His gaze moved over the group, weighing each gesture, each passing shadow, his hand resting near his pistol. Petersen, equally watchful, studied the animated gathering. Their caution, however, proved needless.

The laughter and convivial sounds were a vibrant tapestry woven with threads of simple joys and unburdened existence. It was a paradox, these rugged individuals' lively nature flourishing in the arctic wilderness's harsh embrace. It made Kane and Petersen ponder the resilience of the human spirit; here, surrounded by the relentless, cold arms of nature, lived people, singing the songs of their souls, unbroken, undiminished.

Kane and Petersen moved deeper into the encampment with each measured step, their senses tuned to every nuance of life around them. They were no longer draped in the shadows of fear towards the Esquimaux but instead walked with a blend of curiosity and openness, eager to understand more about the lives and ways of their icy realm inhabitants. The presence of the unknown no longer yielded unease but instead unfurled a potential tapestry of connections amidst the icy shadows.

The Esquimaux, oblivious to the cold, sat unprotected, sheltered only by a bank of mossy rock on one side of the rocky beach. Their huts were mainly deserted, the walls and roofs seemingly falling in, and the windows open to the air. Everything in the settlement seemed to sit out on the rocks.

They were reminiscent of the wildest gypsies, their environment a cacophony of raucous laughter and squalls, interspersed with snores, while their bodies engaged in unrestrained frolicking. Some were gnawing at bird skins, while others were boiling numerous Auks in large stone pots. Two youngsters, their voices amplified in shouts of "Oopegsoak," were in a skirmish over a cooked owl.

The fires, fed with peat moss mixed with bird fat, served only for cooking, warmth being sought in close company. At the center sat old Kresut, the blind patriarch, presiding over the bustle. .

Little ones meandered through, ferrying moss, their innocent faces marked with streaks of grease and blood and morsels of raw liver peeking from between their teeth. It was a living, breathing canvas depicting the essence of raw, unadulterated life and survival, each moment a snapshot of existence in its most primal form.

Birds were plentiful, nesting in the refuse-filled coves beneath the cliffs. Armed with a purse net at the end of a narwhal tusk, two boys would return within minutes, arms laden with as many Auks as they could hold. Dogs, securely tethered to avoid theft and brawls, were well-fed. The atmosphere was one of surplus and relaxation, thoughts of the approaching harsh winter seemingly absent from their minds.

When the veil of night fell within the confines of one of the makeshift huts, Sip-su, the spouse of Marsumah, extended her welcome to the men. She, who had assumed the role of the inaugural "witch" of the cauldron outside, was a presence of warmth in the cramped space. Navigating through a dense weave of inhabitants, Kane reached her and graciously accepted her offer of a bird-skin kapetah to serve as a blanket. With maternal gentleness, she positioned her two-year-old child beneath Kane's head, offering an improvised pillow.

Meanwhile, Petersen secured his own kapetah and settled on a flat rock, contorting his body to fit the hard surface. Kane assimilated with the Esquimaux, partaking in their meal with an adaptive spirit, his actions a subtle mix of respect and participation in the customs of his hosts. The hut, a microcosm of intertwined lives and warmth, buzzed with subdued murmurs and the sound of communal existence in the icy enclave.

The next morning, Marsumah and others from the group bid farewell to the men, furnishing them with a fresh team of dogs. In a transaction steeped in disparity, they claimed Kane's team in return, barring Toodla and Whitey, whom Kane invariably retained as his lead dogs. The sledge was laden with an ample supply of bird meat.

As they drove their load over the ice, Kane's thoughts remained with his men, who, at that moment, were struggling with loads teetering on the brink of their physical capacities, navigating through a boundless terrain of chaotic ice. Each yard they advanced was a testament to their relentless perseverance, their bodies bending and pushing against the overwhelming weight as they etched their paths across the frozen wasteland. The air was punctuated with their muted grunts and the crunching symphony of ice under the relentless press of time and duty.

On the expanses of the ice near Littleton Island, Kane and Petersen found themselves at the mercy of a gale; it bore the essence and might of a cyclone, thrusting forcefully at their backs. It had enough power to topple the dogs, leaving them struggling on their sides against the violent gusts. In several instances, both men were compelled to hurl themselves onto their stomachs to avoid being swept away by the tempest's unforgiving whirl. The storm's uproar rendered communication between them a nearly unattainable feat, their voices lost in the chaotic symphony of the howling winds.

"The ice is collapsing!" Petersen yelled, his voice straining against the whirlwind around them.

"We must move or die!" Kane shouted back, his voice laden with resolve.

"For the salvation of our men, we must make our way back to the boats. Let's move!"

"If they're even still there!" came Petersen's grim retort amidst the roaring gale.

With the storm wailing around them, they forged ahead, battling against the tumult.

Reaching the sledge party with the gale at their backs, Kane, Petersen, and the dogs found the ice firm and the boats intact. The ice party had overturned the craft, set their prows to windward, and lashed them to the ice with whale lines. Blocks of ice braced each hull, leaving space beneath for shelter. The Hope, most exposed to the wind, lay already buried in snow.

With weary bodies, Kane and Petersen slipped beneath one of the overturned vessels, the dogs following closely behind. Beneath the three vessels, all hands found shelter.

"Welcome back," said Brooks, his tone mingling relief with concern. "We have been anxious about the ice."

"It holds," Kane replied. "We are spent. Give us two hours' rest, then we move the boats again."

Old Nessark

Three hours later, the men were in harness, pulling the boats that were now rigged with sails, the steering oar serving as a boom. Old Nessark, with Wilson and Whipple, the last of the invalids, arrived to join the others.

"Easy with the sails!" Kane shouted over the howling wind, his voice straining. "And secure the invalids properly!"

The ill were loaded into the boats, reuniting the group once more. The wind, having shifted to the north, aided in accelerating their pace.

"We have to keep up this pace!" Petersen yelled, veins protruding on his forehead. "Get out ahead and cut through the hummocks! We move as one!"

The group reached the Pekiutlik settlement on the way to Etah, deciding it was a suitable location to stop for the night.

"Let's stop here!" McGary declared, his eyes scanning the settlement.

Once the journey paused, they sat on makeshift seats crafted from boxes to partake in their meal.

"I smell open water," asserted Kane, nostrils slightly flaring.

"We're approaching it," McGary concurred. "But look at that ice—thin, treacherous."

"Dispatch men to test the ice," Kane ordered, determination resonating in his tone.

Approaching Etah, the Inuit extended their aid. They hauled ropes, transported the ailing, and provided auks.

"How much further?" one of the men asked.

"Not far now," Kane replied, a glimmer of hope in his eyes. "We push on."

The men and Inuit worked together, their voices merging in a harmonious tumult as they approached Etah.

They halted for the night just south of Etah, near open water, sheltered behind a ridge of packed ice that blocked their way.

"Just another challenge," Kane said, his gaze locked onto the barriers ahead.

"And one we'll overcome," Petersen responded, clenching his fists, his eyes shining with unwavering resolve.

"I've come to recognize each one," said Kane, his gaze surveying the playful frolic. "There's Metek and Nualik, Myouk and Sievu, Accomodah, Nessark with Anak, his wife, Marsinga with Aningna, Tellerk with Amaunalik, Sip-su with Marsumah, and his little daughter, Aningnah."

"It's like beholding a cohesive family in a foreign land, enriched with fellowship, tranquility, and, at times, with nourishment," Hayes contemplated, absorbing the surrounding vibrancy of life.

"Yes—only six months ago they faced the threat of starvation," Kane said. "Yet the shadow of what lay ahead never dimmed their spirits, then or now."

"It seems to be woven into their being," mused Hayes. "The relentless unpredictability here seems to make them more aligned with living in the present—a paradigm of resilience and joyful existence, something we ought to assimilate."

Beside the tent, Sip-su's little daughter, Aningnah, wept softly, wiping her eyes with a bird-skin. Kane felt an affinity for these beings—unclean, despondent, yet blissful—who had been long-standing neighbors and, more recently, steadfast friends. Around them, women tended their cooking, infants cried, and men conversed in animated tones, their talk often breaking into laughter.

"They've spared us several days' labor in reaching the water's edge," Hayes observed.

"We're at such a late stage in the season that even slight aid could be the pivot on which our survival turns," Kane acknowledged.

"Have you taken note?" inquired Hayes. "Previously, our predominant apprehension was their potential pilfering, but now, with all our valuables strewn across the ice, not a single item has gone missing."

"They're embodiments of the present," responded Kane. "Their lack of want translates to a lack of worry about future needs. Their survival hinges on cooperation and sharing. Those are the lessons we need to internalize."

"We have grown much like them," Hayes noted.

"Even more significantly," concurred Kane, "we've intertwined our destinies. We have become part of their family, ingrained as Esquimaux for eternity."

The following morning, the men stowed their tents and furs in the boats. The inhabitants of Etah, in their entirety, assembled to bid them farewell. High up on the adjacent hillside, Kane's eyes fell upon Hans, standing next to a young, expectant Esquimaux woman, both watching the pre-departure bustle. Kane subtly drew a few men's attention towards Hans, alerting the rest to his presence. A wave from Hans was reciprocated with waves from the group. Then, Hans casually strolled away with his arm around his companion. At the same time, on a distant elevation to the left, two polar bears, one large and one small, also turned and ambled away.

"In the eternal circle of life, in time, all young men leave their mother's nest to make their own," Kane mused.

With deliberate motions, Kane released Toodla and Whitey from their team and handed their leads to Petersen, gesturing towards the boats. The leads of the remaining dogs were entrusted to Metek. Additionally, he distributed items no longer needed, such as knives, needles, and other items, as parting gifts.

"In our thanks," Kane said in halting Esquimaux, "we leave you these. We go now to our snow-houses beyond the great sea."

A brief exchange of puzzled glances unfolded amongst them, followed by a realization which initiated with one and soon resonated through waves from the others.

XXIII. Leaving Etah

Saying Goodbye

From Etah, the crew toiled a full day to reach the ice edge. Once there, they labored to lift the boats over the ridge of piled pack ice, launching the 'Red Eric' first. Kane retrieved the Marston rifle from it, giving it a quick, appraising glance before handing it to Godfrey.

Simultaneously, Kane and McGary cast their eyes skyward.

"Rapidly approaching gale, rising seas," McGary noted tersely. "Maybe we should delay."

"We cannot spare a day," Kane responded firmly.

"All aboard, who's goin' aboard!" Brooks yelled.

Cheers erupted from the men.

The crossing neared Southerland Island, and as forewarned, the sea lay tumultuous and shadowed, its surface a chaotic chop. Kane and his crew had forsaken the calm of familiar surroundings for threading a delicate balance between an imperious sea and their fragile vessels. It was a razor's edge of existence—every pulse of nature's untamed force poised to usher them into deliverance or doom hung on the slightest tremor of nature's force and what little they could do to help each other.

Adjacent to the island, barricaded by an impenetrable embrace of ice, leaving no hope to haul the boats ashore, Kane carefully climbed from the 'Hope' onto the precarious ice-belt. His mission was clear, albeit fraught with risk—fill their large kettle with snow to convert into life-sustaining water.

The air was laden with unspoken tension, every crunch of his boots on the snow echoing as a subdued omen. The collected snow spoke silently of the untamed wilderness around them, gently reminding them of their transient passage through this frozen landscape. With caution, he resumed his position in the boat, the kettle full of snow, every motion a careful balance between living and the chilling clasp of the sea.

The 'Red Eric' was beleaguered by the turbulent waves, with the only visible land receding into the distance. The 'Faith' adeptly drew close on the starboard side of the 'Red Eric,' aiming to shield it from the relentless waves and the piercing spray, while the 'Hope' mirrored the protective maneuver on the port side.

Amid the chaos, Riley, Petersen, and Bonsall struggled to clamber into the 'Hope.' The battle against the raging sea was fierce, but they succeeded, even though the violent waters rendered the transfer of cargo unattainable. Amidst the turmoil, Petersen managed to fasten the 'Red Eric' behind the 'Hope,' preparing it to be towed through the furious sea.

Soon, the 'Hope' was in distress. Towing the 'Red Eric' slowed her progress, each wave a mounting challenge.

"Brooks, we're shipping water faster than we can bail," Kane shouted, his voice sharp against the storm. "We can't take this sea abeam. Find an opening in the ice pack to starboard!"

A robust sheet of ice held firm to their right, a stark barrier against the wind-whipped sea.

Upon reaching the ice, the boats anchored within a slender inlet in the flow. The men, succumbing to exhaustion, settled into sleep, layering blankets over furs beside their vessels on the icy ground. The lingering fatigue robbed them of the strength to haul the boats from the water— a task that demanded attention. In each boat, a man stayed vigilant, focused on bailing, and ready to alert the others should the ice show any sign of shifting.

They sought refuge for a day on the ice before facing several days of rowing through moderate seas, their eyes fixed on a small, distant island. As they drew nearer to the island, they found themselves amidst a large field of shattered ice. While the three boats were carefully maneuvering through openings in the densely packed ice, Kane, who had held his post at the helm for sixteen exhaustive hours, collapsed. McGary immediately took command while Kane slept at the bottom of the 'Hope.'

After navigating a winding path through leads for several grueling hours, they encountered an area interspersed with colossal icebergs.

"Anchor us in the shelter of that closest berg; we need to rest and brew some tea," instructed McGary. Noticing Kane stirring, he inquired, "How are you holding up?"

"Much improved," Kane responded, his voice steady. "Tea will mitigate the impact of our dwindling rations as well. Once you've rested, we'll climb the berg to survey what lies ahead."

"Dwindling rations?" McGary raised an eyebrow.

"Yes, rations must be pared down to the bare minimum," confirmed Kane.

"Navigating through this pack ice is proving more strenuous than anticipated," McGary remarked, his tone edged with concern. "Our stamina will wane with reduced rations."

Kane gave him a look.

"But, of course, prudence necessitates it; other delays may be unavoidable," McGary said, catching Kane's drift.

"Six ounces of bread-dust blended with a morsel of tallow, about the size of a walnut, in a concoction of paste— that should suffice," articulated Kane. McGary directed a playful, teasing gaze at Kane. "You'll— ah— spread it out uniformly throughout the day for us?" McGary asked—a note of mischief in his tone. "Assuredly," replied Kane, his lips curling into a reassuring smile.

An hour later, while the boats remained tethered to the berg, Kane and McGary climbed to its summit. When they returned, Petersen asked, "What's the outlook?"

"Indeed, the winter has been relentless and the summer fleeting," Kane disclosed. "Our view reveals nothing but an endless expanse of unyielding ice."

"By the heavens, we should see open water and the spout of whales, not this frozen sea," McGary lamented..

Silence swept over the men as they retreated into their blankets, surrendering to slumber.

Days deepened within the flow, and a harsh gale engulfed the three small boats amid the vast expanse of ice. The drift was forcibly pressing against the rocky shores of Greenland's northern coast. The floating cake ice encircling their vessels spanned miles in every direction, commencing a slow, ominous rotation around some unseen fulcrum. It started to close in on their slender refuge with unrelenting force. Initially, the floe submitted to the gusts, crashing into the jagged coastal rocks.

Suddenly confronted by anchored ice from the north, a catastrophic transformation unfolded instantaneously. Enormous, fragmented ice sheets, each three feet thick or more, were upheaved, creating chaotic ramparts around the helpless men as the entire icy realm succumbed to the tempest's impact. The collision and contraction resonated in an overpowering cacophony that Kane's vocal orders dissipated into the turmoil. The men, driven by instinct, stayed at their stations, but getting freed was a vanishing hope. This ice attack wasn't a benign pinch; their sturdy Advance would have seemed a feeble contraption amidst the overpowering ice structures, let alone their small boats, which appeared as fragile as splinters. The encompassing icy stage where the boats lay was subjected to wild disintegration and chaotic reshuffling under the relentless assault.

The boats, laden with men and supplies, were jolted and elevated, twirled in the air by forces unimaginable amidst a clamor so indomitable that not even the combined roars of a thousand trumpets could pierce through. The 'Faith' sustained a blow to her starboard but maintained her integrity despite the brutal contact.

Suddenly, silence fell, ending the upheaval as swiftly as it had begun. The boats, adrift among churning ice and snow, lay miraculously intact yet wholly at the mercy of the elements. The men exchanged brief, searching glances—an unspoken acknowledgment of the spectacle they had just survived.

After more than a day of uncertainty, the boats were finally drawn alongside the belt ice. At the next high tide, the men stepped ashore and scaled the ice-cliff. With great exertion, they dragged the boats onto a narrow shelf, working in unison. Too spent to unload their cargo, they paused—startled to see the sky thick with eiders.

"It must be a breeding ground," Whipple said.

"Oh boy, eggs!" Hickey shouted.

Speaking of the birds, they soon succumbed to exhaustion and slept where they sat.

After a deep sleep, they began gathering eggs at twelve hundred per day. Once the storm abated, they dried bird meat on the rocks and stowed their treasure when the storms raged again. At times, snow fell heavily. The boats and the men remained sheltered with their backs against the same rocks that sheltered the eiders.

"I can hardly believe yesterday's ordeal," Kane said.

"Who can explain how we ended up afloat after that upheaval?" Bonsall asked.

"When the 'Faith' was stove-in, I expected men to die," Brooks said.

"Yet we survived again," Bonsall replied.

"This deserves a celebration," Kane said. "Mr. Bonsall, fix up some patriotic eggnog, and we'll spice it up with our remaining medicinal alcohol flask."

"You have been keeping this from us?" Bonsall asked, smiling.

A cheer went up. Bonsall cracked eggs into a kettle while Brooks fetched powdered milk and Kane's medical kit from the boat. One by one, the men joined in, adding their eggs to the kettle.

After days of respite and recovery, the time came to depart the encasing ice cliff. The mission unfolded with challenges; as they lowered their boats off the rugged ice, the 'Hope' slipped from the grips of the weary men, plunging fervently into the sludge beneath, caving in its rail and bulwark. Many indispensable items spilled overboard, including their cherished kettle and the shotgun, which Bonsall had placed therein temporarily, were among the lost. The boat itself clung to existence, narrowly evading destruction. An additional day of strenuous efforts was needed to mend her wounds and redistribute the loads.

When the three battered boats were eventually relaunched, ready to transport their human partners, Kane pulled McGary into a hushed conference.

"I hate to say this," Kane said. "It may come down to sacrificing Toodla and Whitey soon."

"I'd hate to see it after all they did for us," McGary said. "Even now, they continue to help us by carrying their own fat."

Kane felt a deep bond with Toodla, who had once saved his life. Yet the weight of his duty to the men pressed harder than sentiment, and the thought lay heavy on his heart.

XXIV. Scarcity & Loss

Approximately a week later, they reached a new, isolated, and desolate destination: Cape York enveloped in a fog that was almost lyrical in its mystery. They established their camp on a rocky, albeit forgiving, shore that afforded the boats a more gracious landing. With a chart unfolded before him, Kane consulted with Brooks and McGary as they drew near.

"We're down to six hundred and fifty pounds of rations," Brooks announced, the worry evident in his voice.

"That's only thirty-six pounds per man—it won't see us through a week," Kane calculated, his tone heavy with the weight of their predicament.

"We must tighten our belts further and hunt down some meat." "We have but one rifle cartridge left," McGary added, with a sense of urgency in his voice.

"Fuel is nearly exhausted as well," Brooks pointed out. "Considering the peat-like turf found by Hickey, the spare oars, our figurehead Augusta, and an empty cask, we might make it last fifteen days. With the Red Eric and the empty provision bags added, we could possibly push it to twenty-one days. However, progress is imperative."

"No time for delays," asserted Kane. "I'll survey the ice ahead."

"I'll ready the men and boats," Brooks replied swiftly.

The boats were rapidly launched into the water.

"Fortune seems to be favoring us," remarked Kane. "A clear and definite lead, slicing through the outer floes, stretches out to sea as far as the eyes can perceive."

"And the fuel, what of it?" queried Brooks.

"Reassign the cargo of the Red Eric among the remaining boats, then dismantle her. Adjust the crew as deemed necessary."

Shrouded in the coming darkness and adrift among the floes, McGary roused Kane from his sleep in the sheltered bow of the Faith.

"The pilot has led us astray," McGary uttered in hushed tones.

"Our path has altered?" Kane asked quietly, his voice laden with the remnants of sleep.

"Misled by the track of a colossal iceberg, he has abandoned the principal lead," McGary whispered.

"Our scant provisions cannot bear such waste," Kane said gravely. "We must turn back."

At the rudder beside McGary, he kept his eyes fixed ahead.

"The pack is encroaching upon our slender waterway," McGary noted solemnly. "Both receding and proceeding seem unviable."

"Say nothing to the crew," Kane murmured. "Have the boats hauled ashore and camp made—tell them it is to dry our gear."

McGary, Kane's steadfast second officer and long seasoned in the hardships of whaling, felt his eyes sting. Passing the order to Godfrey in the next boat, he crawled beneath the canvas to cover the stores and quietly rouse the resting men.

Hours later, out on the ice in their leather rue-raddies, the men strained to haul the boats on runners along a narrow lead. At last, they reached a broader opening, just as a north wind began to rise. The boats were relaunched under ragged sails, the runners left lashed beneath them for want of strength to remove them.

Following the lead brought them only faintly within sight of land.

Kane scrutinized his compass. "We have but eight days' fuel, and less in provisions," Brooks said gravely.

"Scant indeed," Kane agreed.

"Our sightings amount to a few stray birds, no game, and one wary seal," McGary said.

"We still have tea—our one true comfort," Brooks added.

"Rations must be cut to three ounces of bread-dust, one of tallow, and two of bird-meat," Kane ordered.

"We might follow the coast for game, though it would be slow, or strike directly across the open sea," Godfrey proposed.

"It is a gamble," Kane mused, "but it could save us days. We must take it."

Soon, they found themselves again traversing waters unseen from land. Surrounded by a gentle mist and ensconced within the external pack, fractured leads were visible in multiple directions. Kane resolved that they had to pull up onto the drifting ice.

Most of the men re-experienced respiratory issues and swelling they had encountered on the Advance. Hickey, seeking relief, slit open his canvas boots.

In low tones, McGary said to Kane, "The shortcut is proving vain, is it not?"

"It is," conceded Kane. "We've drifted twenty miles northward. The concept was sound until the elements turned against us."

"The men long for the safety of the shore," McGary observed.

"Our course stands," Kane replied. "We launch again, steering south as the leads permit, and look east for a break in the pack."

Brooks approached them. "The crew can't endure the scant rations much longer," he declared. "Their strength is rapidly diminishing."

"We have our 'meat on the hoof,'" reminded Kane. "They will serve soon enough."

Every ounce of the men's bodily reserves and even some of their muscle had been consumed. Their mechanical, stiff, and abrupt movements were propelled more by their unwavering resolve than by their scant nourishment—a determination surpassing human endurance's conceivable boundaries.

XXV. Last Bullet

They pushed through the icy expanse of the Atlantic, their worn boats demanding constant bailing and repair. The cold pressed in, silent and unyielding. McGary suddenly spotted a large seal asleep on the ice to starboard.

With quiet urgency, McGary signaled to Kane. In turn, Kane motioned for the 'Faith' to take the lead, with 'Hope' following closely. The air was thick with worry as Petersen, joined by Godfrey in the 'Faith,' grabbed the Marston rifle and took his place in the bow while Godfrey steered with steady hands.

Petersen reached into his pocket and pulled out a rifle shell—their last one. This chance was their last to stave off starvation. The two dogs would last only a few more days, yet they were still ten to twenty miles from any settlement. A missed shot would mean ruin.

The air was thick with silence, each breath a pale cloud. Hearts quickened as they balanced between hope and despair, their fate resting on a single bullet.

Two men fastened stockings over the oar locks, silencing the oars. They neared the animal. The palpable tension made each stroke a silent struggle. At three hundred yards, Kane signaled; oars were drawn in, and Morton quietly took over, sculling astern.

The seal lifted its head as they came within range. Kane glanced at his men—faces worn with fatigue—as it stirred. Their survival hinged on this moment. With a steady hand, Kane signalled Petersen to fire. McGary ceased sculling, and the boat drifted closer.

Godfrey, observing Petersen, saw his paralyzing anxiety. Silently, he steadied the rifle on the boat's cutwater. The seal, sensing danger, prepared to dive but relaxed at the rifle's crack.

With no bullet left, Kane could only watch as discipline frayed. Shouts rang out as the men rushed toward the floe.

Arriving, they saw the seal slipping away. "It'll sink!" warned Morton.

"Oh, God!" exclaimed Petersen.

Godfrey plunged into the freezing water, stopping the seal's slide. He heaved it up just enough for the others to drag it clear of its hole.

Behind Kane, the men, half-crazed, seized the seal and pulled it to safer ice, reduced as they were from absolute famine.

Kane, Brooks, and McGary hurried to assist Godfrey, knowing the danger. The ice around them was still treacherous, and the cold was overtaking him. Kane reached out while McGary lay prone, holding fast to his ankles. Godfrey's strength faltered, his grip slipping—then, for a moment, they caught hold in a desperate struggle.

Locking eyes with Kane, Godfrey released his grip with a resigned nod and succumbed to the depths, a silent savior and forever the leader he wanted to be for the men he had left behind.

The men endured for twelve more grueling days, navigating their boats across seas cluttered with ice. They lived off what remained of Godfrey's seal, sparingly using fuel to melt ice for water. When they were left with only two dogs for food and considering burning Augusta for fuel, a turn of fate occurred.

Laboring through thick fog, they suddenly came face to face with a slow-moving fishing trawler from the northernmost port, Fiskernaes, narrowly avoiding a collision. Their sudden appearance next to the trawler startled the fishermen on board. The crew appeared as skeletons emerging from the mist to the fishermen.

It was a close call, but they were saved.

XXVI. Return Home

A few days later, after a modest period of recuperation on a ship moored in the harbor, the men found themselves at a gathering hosted by the local governor, welcoming them back to the realms of civilization. The governor's abode was a beacon of civility and comfort—luxuries the men hadn't known for over two years.

Standing in a daze amid the murmurs and laughter of the ballroom, Kane suddenly found himself jolted back to the present as a hand was being withdrawn from his. The governor's assistant had been extending a greeting.

He became aware of Henri Bellow's presence, immersed in quiet conversation with a few men nearby. A drink found its way into Kane's hand, offered silently by the assistant. The men turned to Kane.

"Fine job, surviving and finding your way back to Fiskernaes again," a man said. "A pity it was all for nothing—Henri Bellow found evidence of Sir Franklin's party some five hundred miles southwest of where you froze in, near Newfoundland, was it not?"

"I believe so," Kane said, distracted as he walked away.

Admiral Hall arrived with several Navy officers. The officers drifted away as the admiral approached Kane after accepting a drink from the host.

"You led your brave men back well," the admiral said.

"Thank you, admiral," Kane said. "You've come to congratulate Henri, I imagine. A well-deserved honor."

"We are fortunate to have the opportunity to congratulate you both," he said. "Is there anything I can do for you?"

Kane thought for a moment.

"Yes, for something one of the men did," Kane said.

"Name it," the admiral said.

"I would like you to give William Godfrey a posthumous commission promoting him to captain," Kane said. "He sacrificed his life to save us all."

"As soon as I reach my office, it will be done," the admiral said.

Kane could not remain within four walls without an oppressive sense of suffocation and stifling warmth. Kane put his untouched drink on a table and slipped out the patio door into the night.

He walked over to a sloping snowbank, sat down, leaned against it, and gazed at the stars. The cold on his back felt comfortable. As he lost himself in thought, two white paws, like those of a small bear, appeared at the top of the snowbank behind his head, akin to when the bear jumped Godfrey. Suddenly, Toodla bounded over the crest to greet Kane with kisses, followed closely by Whitey and McGary. McGary slid down beside Kane as the dogs settled at their feet.

"The men are sicker now in comfort than they were at Etah," McGary said. "Shall we ever grow used to an indoor climate again?"

"Do we wish to think of the future?" Kane asked. "Or simply take what pleasure we can in the present?"

"All our effort and Bellot finds Franklin with a fraction of the effort," McGary said. "What did we accomplish?"

"We brought home every man we could; may Baker and Pierre rest in peace," Kane said. "We learned how wise the Esquimaux are. We reached farther north than any man before and survived two winters in the most extreme environment mankind has known."

"We learned to live like the Esquimaux, too," McGary said.

"Are you taking something home to remind you to live in the present?" Kane asked.

"Augusta!" McGary exclaimed. "Will you take the dogs?"

"If you insist," Kane said. "They can always be used as 'meat on the hoof.'"

That night, Riley snuck onto another ship.

The End

The Advance Remained Behind

PostScript

The wreck of HMS Erebus was discovered in September 2014 in Queen Maud Gulf, off King William Island, in the Canadian Arctic Archipelago—far west of where Kane and the Advance had ventured. In September 2016, HMS Terror was found in Terror Bay, off the island's southwest coast. Lying thirty-two miles apart, the sites suggest one ship was lost before the other attempted to sail south toward mainland Canada, only to fall short.

The discovery of the wrecks has offered invaluable insight into the fate of the Franklin Expedition, enabling researchers to examine the remains and artifacts that shed light on the crew's final days and the conditions they endured while trapped in the Arctic ice. The exact sequence of events leading to their demise remains the subject of ongoing study. Kane's fate was far more fortunate.

Lastly, amidst the Esquimaux, Kane observed a charity most profound—the unerring devotion they bestowed upon one another and even upon strangers, enabling survival in the world's most severe conditions. Indeed, we might all embrace a more harmonious existence by extending such mutual aid, particularly within our gentler climates.

ALSO BY CHARLES PATTON

• For Honest Citizens Only

A bold call for Americans to rise above politics and rebuild civic integrity.

• In Defense of the Righteous

A gripping story of moral courage when justice and survival collide.

• Tigers of the Ice

Adventure meets survival in an unforgiving world where instinct rules.

• Mastering Strategy

The essential guide to thinking, planning, and winning in any field.

• Thinking

Learn how to think more clearly, act decisively, and change your life.

• Artificial Consciousness

Explores the frontier of automating consciousness.

• The Gardener's Secret and Other Stories

Mysteries and dramas revealing the hidden motives behind ordinary lives.

• Extreme Leadership

What real leaders do when the stakes are high.

• Who Do You Trust

A deadly game of deceit between two spies and one truth.

• Busted, What's Wrong With My Excuse

An entertaining look at excuses people make, and how to excuse better.

• Naked Reflections

Raw, honest poetry of truth, ego, and the search for authenticity.

• Charles Patton, Visionaire

Insights from a lifetime of ideas, invention, and fearless creativity.

• Storming the Castle Bridge

A tale of rebellion, loyalty, and the unbreakable human will to be free.

Find every title at: charlespattonbooks.com